JUDY'S JOURNEY

For
Emma Celeste

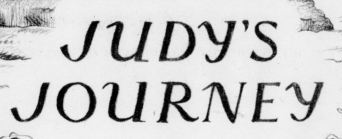

JUDY'S JOURNEY

by

Lois Lenski

1947

J.B. LIPPINCOTT COMPANY
New York and Philadelphia

"A New World Lies Before Us!"

CONTENTS

CHAPTER		PAGE
I.	ALABAMA	1
II.	FLORIDA	15
III.	THE LITTLE LAKE	29
IV.	THE MIDDLE-SIZED LAKE	45
V.	THE BIG LAKE	60
VI.	THE CANAL BANK	74
VII.	BEAN TOWN	90
VIII.	OLEANDER	108
IX.	GEORGIA	123
X.	THE CAROLINAS	139
XI.	VIRGINIA	156
XII.	DELAWARE	171
XIII.	NEW JERSEY	187
XIV.	JOURNEY'S END	200

Map
showing crops
along
Atlantic Seaboard
harvested
by Migrants,
and Route taken
by the
Drummond family~

Foreword

Americans have always been on the go since they first left the Old World and came to the New. They came to get land. They migrated westward, and still farther westward, looking always for land. They went west, found the land they wanted, and putting down their roots, founded our Nation. It has been an American tradition that a man has a right to own a piece of land for himself.

In recent years, the automobile has given rise to a modern migration. But this one is of a different kind. Families are being forced off the land, either because of the impossibility of making a living there, or because machinery has taken the place of man power. The number of homeless migrants, living under conditions which make impossible normal participation in the benefits of American life, is so large that it is a matter for grave concern.

When I read the manuscript of this book to a group of Seventh Grade boys and girls in a small Connecticut manufacturing city, they were surprised to learn that there are any poor children in the United States—children so poor they haven't money enough to go to a movie. They did not know that there are children in our country without shoes, proper clothing and food, and even without homes. Many adults do not know it either.

And yet there are thousands of migrant families, traveling in shabby automobiles for long distances in the Far West, the Middle West, and in the East, to get poorly paying and quickly ending jobs. They follow the crops—beans, cotton, potatoes, prunes, sugar beets, berries and fruits—at their harvest season, and help with the picking. Whenever you eat beans or peas from a can, remember that a child may have spent long hours in the sun, picking them for you.

The individual owner or the company who raises these crops on a large scale, is dependent upon outside workers coming in, because when the crop is ready, it must be picked immediately or it will be ruined. Some growers have provided adequate housing for this extra help, others none at all, so the pickers live the best way they can. When the crop is over, they "move on" to another crop. The United States Government has provided camps for migrants in certain areas, but these have not been adequate to meet the needs.

The Children's Bureau of the U. S. Dept. of Labor says: "Hundreds of thousands of children—some as young as six—follow the crops with their families and work in the fields to help produce the food we eat." These migrant children exist with only the bare necessities of life. Many of them do not go to school at all, others go for a few months a year, if the family stays in one place long enough. In the communities where they stop, they are often looked upon as aliens and therefore undesirable, and are given little or no chance to share in community life. A large number are white children, others are Negro or Mexican-American or other nationalities.

I have seen and talked to migrant children and heard them tell of their experiences. One girl of eleven picked twenty-two hampers (half-bushel baskets) of beans in a day; a seven-year-old picked five hampers. They go to the field at six in the morning and return at dark. They have never had books or playthings. Some of them are no longer childlike, but are already old before they are ten. They do not know how to play—they are good fighters.

Everything in their life is against them. As one migrant-teacher told me: "They have never had a break. And yet they are brave, courageous, full of spirit, and anxious to learn. They respond so quickly to all you do for them. They have had so little—every thing you do for them means so much." In this teacher's class, the migrant children are making democracy work. Here mountain white and

FOREWORD

Northern white, Southern Negro, Japanese-American and American children of foreign descent are living and learning together, peacefully and happily.

The Home Missions Council is doing good work among the migrants by providing health centers, child care centers, religious counseling and inter-faith church services. Their work was begun on the Atlantic seaboard in 1920 and was extended in a few years to the West Coast and then to the Middle West.

The characters in my book are imaginary, but the incidents used are taken from the experiences of living migrants. I am deeply indebted to the National Child Labor Committee and to the Home Missions Council for their generous provision of migratory material and for their invaluable counsel in helping me to present an accurate and truthful picture of the migrants.

The Song, You Are My Sunshine, the chorus of which I have quoted, is copyright 1940—Peer International Corporation. Used by Permission.

Lois Lenski

Greenacres,
Harwinton, Connecticut
October 27, 1946

"I am a part of all that I have met."

A great English poet, Tennyson, once wrote this of a man, Ulysses, who had been all over the world and met many kinds of people, and seen how they worked and lived. And so we too are a part of all that we have met. Each person that we meet teaches us something that can make us kinder and more understanding of the people of our own country and the world.

CHAPTER I

Alabama

"HEY! Anybody home?"

A ten-year-old girl, big eyes in a pale face and stringy hair hanging loose on her shoulders, peered out of the open door. She wore overalls and her feet were bare.

A cold wind blew round the corner.

"What you want?" asked the girl in a frightened whisper.

"Where's your Pa?" asked the big man who stood there.

"Gone off," said the girl. "Don't know where."

The man did not offer to come in. Through the open door of the rickety, unpainted cabin, he could see that the place was empty. The walls inside were papered with old newspapers. Dirt and refuse covered the floor. The sight was unpleasant, so he turned away.

Outside, there wasn't much to see either. The house sat in the middle of a cotton field, where the dried stalks of dead cotton plants leaned crazily against each other. Splotches of white were sprinkled over them, mute evidence of a ruined unpicked crop. There were no farm buildings, no trees, no bushes—there was no green grass.

The man's car was in the narrow dirt lane that led in from the road. In front of the car stood a pile of furniture, heaped carelessly together.

"Ain't you folks got out yet? What you hangin' round for?" the man asked in a loud voice. "Come on out—no use your hidin' in there."

The girl had disappeared. A scuffle was heard inside and a woman came to the door, holding a baby in her arms. She was thin and pale, her straight hair rolled in a knot on her head. Her eyes were soft and patient.

"Howdy, Mister Reeves," she said in a dull voice.

"I done tole him Papa was gone off and we don't know where," said the girl, appearing again with a younger girl beside her.

"I see Moses and Smoky moved your plunder out like I told 'em, Miz Drummond," said Reeves.

"Shore did," said the woman. "We're jest puttin' our vittles in a basket, sir. . . . We're most ready to go. . . ."

"Well, I can't wait all day," said Reeves. "I give you-all your orders."

The girl stepped forward.

[2]

"Now, Judy," said her mother, "don't you say nary word to rile Mister Reeves."

But Judy did not listen. She faced the man and said: "I reckon you think you own the whole world!" She set her bare feet on the rickety step and stuck out her tongue.

"I'm overseer for the Company," boomed Reeves. "It's my job to make this land pay. I intend to put some one on it can take care of it, make the crops and make 'em pay!"

"You can have your ole fields and your ole cotton and your little ole piecy house as full of holes as a sieve and welcome!" snapped Judy. "But you can't have the sun nor the blue sky nor the moon 'n' stars, nor the sunset, so there!"

"I notice you-all got plenty time to set and study the sunset," said Reeves. "Plenty time to set and do nothin'. Your Pa had plenty time to go huntin' and fishin', with cotton bustin' open right under his nose——"

"Where's my puppy dog?"

The sharp cry came from a boy who dashed round the house. He doubled up his thin little fists at the man. "What you done with my little ole puppy dog?"

"I told you you couldn't keep a dog on this place," answered Reeves, "and I'd run it off the farm if you brung it here."

"My Uncle Barney give it to me. . . ." The boy began to whimper. "He said I could keep it for my very own. . . ."

"What you done with Joe Bob's dog?" asked Mrs. Drummond in a fretful tone. "You ain't harmed the little bitty thing, have you, Mist' Reeves? The boy set such store by it, it'll cut him to pieces if you——"

"You jest went and killed it, I betcha!" said Judy. "You jest *like* to be mean. You're the hatefullest man this side o' Kingdom Come!"

Mister Reeves eyed the girl fiercely, backed away and said nothing.

"He ain't *said* he hurt your dog, sonny," said Mama. Joe Bob began to cry.

"Come on, git out o' the house!" roared Reeves. "I'm sick of the lot of ye. Come on outdoors, you-all!"

"What's outdoors? What's the blue sky to us, even in wintertime?" said Mama. "We been livin' outdoors, what with all them big holes in the roof. Rain always leakin' through—I'm plumb tard o' movin' the bed every night to keep it out of the wet. All that terrible rain——"

"Can ketch a dishpan o' water over the stove ary time it rains," said Judy.

"Holes in the roof big enough to throw a shoe through," said Joe Bob.

"If we jest had some shoes to throw," added Judy.

"Cold winter wind nigh blows the covers offen the bed," said Joe Bob.

"We like to froze to death on them cold nights," said Judy.

"Worstest house I ever seen," said Mama. "We'll leave it and welcome. We can't worst ourselves much by leavin' such a place."

They talked back to Old Man Reeves in loud voices. They took delight in shouting what a bad house it was. But their feet kept moving out of it—reluctantly. They remembered it was all the house they had. Even with holes in the roof and walls, it was home. Even if it didn't keep the winter cold out, it was home.

The baby began to cry.

"Lonnie's sick, my baby boy," said Mama. Mama's voice was not defiant now. It was sad, as if she might start crying too. "No time to be movin' in winter when your baby boy's sick."

"No fault o' mine," said Reeves. "Been tryin' to get you folks out ever since settlement time. Why don't you take care of your kids?"

"Pickin' cotton all day, that's why," answered Mama. "That's when Lonnie first took sick. Nothin' to eat but fatback and cornbread. You wouldn't never let us have a little garden patch." It was true—the cotton field came right up to the house on all sides. Only the narrow lane was unplanted.

"Teacher at school said we should eat garden sass," piped up Judy.

"Teacher said we'd git puny if we didn't," added her sister, little Cora Jane.

"Can't have good cotton land wasted," growled Reeves. "Don't stand there a-talkin' all day. Git on out. I got a new family a-comin' in."

"Lord help 'em!" said Mama.

"Come on then!" ordered Reeves.

They all followed at the man's heels.

"Judy, we left our coats," said Mama. "Go back and fetch 'em, so we don't ketch our death o' cold out here."

The girl went into the house.

"Them kids went to school instead of pickin' cotton?" demanded Reeves. "Didn't I tell Jim Drummond to keep 'em

outa school till pickin' was over? So that's why he didn't get no pickin' done before the rains started!"

Judy handed out the coats and they put them on.

"It rained and rained," the girl said. "It rained so much we couldn't go back to school. The creek was flooded. I wanted to finish the Third Reader——"

"I liked my teacher," said Cora Jane.

" 'Twas rain ruint the cotton," said Mama. "Can't blame it onto us. It rained and we couldn't pick. I'm right smart glad them young uns went to school when they had the chance."

"You want 'em to git new-fangled notions from them teachers, I reckon," said Reeves.

" 'Bout what's good for young uns to eat?" put in Judy. " 'Bout shuttin' up holes in your house to keep out the cold?"

Reeves walked out to the lane where their meager furniture was piled. There was a bureau with a broken mirror, a large iron bed, a table, a kerosene stove, a sewing-machine and various odds and ends. Reeves picked up a small piece of carpet that lay on top of a heap of bedding. He held it out at arm's length.

"Carpet, eh? Brussels carpet! With roses on it. Now what——"

He got no further. Joe Bob, like an enraged animal, jumped up and snatched the carpet out of the man's hand.

"Gimme that or I'll beat the stuffin' out of you!" the boy cried. He dropped the carpet and pounded the man with his fists.

"Git offen me, you little varmint!" shouted Reeves.

Just then the sound of a car could be heard in the neighborhood. The boy stopped fighting and they all looked off across the cotton field. The car was coming closer and closer, rattling and banging louder and louder.

"It's comin' here," said Joe Bob.

"Shore is," said Mama.

"It's Papa!" shrieked Judy.

With arms and legs flying, she was off down the lane. When the car came up, she was sitting in the front seat beside her father. On her face there was a satisfied smile.

"I was tellin' your folks they gotta get out," said Old Man
Reeves as soon as the engine stopped.

"I see," said Jim Drummond. "Moved all our plunder out
too, didn't you?"

"My colored boys done that. Gotta get the house ready for
new family comin' in."

"O. K.," said Jim Drummond. "We're goin' soon as we can
git loaded up. We're goin' where we'll never see the likes o'
you again."

"Oh where, Papa?" cried Judy. Papa looked *happy*. It was
wonderful. Things weren't so bad after all.

"Hush up your mouth, gal," said Papa. He turned to Reeves
again. "We're a-goin' where the sun's a-shinin' and a man can
make a crop of his own. We're lightin' out right away, the
sooner, the better."

Old Man Reeves seemed surprised and taken aback. He had
been expecting an argument and maybe a fight.

"Where you off to, Jim, anyhow?" he asked amiably.
"Where'd you git the car? Latest model, eh? Roby Watson's
got a tenant-house empty, but he won't treat you half as good
as I been doin'. Where you off to?"

Papa just rubbed his chin and said nothing.

"Don't you wisht you knew!" sang out Judy spitefully.
"There's plenty places to go to. It's a free country, I reckon."

Joe Bob and Cora Jane began to dance up and down. "Don't
you wisht you knew! Don't you wisht you knew! It's a free
country, a free country."

Still Papa didn't say a word. His silence made Reeves angry.

"I'd ought to knock you down," the man began slowly, "for the way you've neglected this place and lost me the cotton crop and stole fertilizer and stuff and ain't worked the crops nor kept your part of the bargain. Lookin' to me to feed and clothe you and furnish you medicines for a sick family and then ruinin' the cotton crop."

"I reckon we're about even, Reeves," said Papa in a cold, hard voice. "You know what you been sayin' ain't true. 'Twas the rain ruint the cotton. For three years now I've worked my fingers to the bone for you and what do I get out of it? Nothin'. I'm worse off than when I come here. Mind how I never got that new wagon I wanted? Well, it's over now. I'm through bein' a sharecropper—lucky I got spunk enough left to clear out. Ever since you made away with my boy's puppy dog——"

"Oh Papa! Did he kill it?" Joe Bob began to kick and scream.

"Steady, boy, steady," said Papa. "Cryin' won't bring your puppy dog back. Well, ever since then, I made up my mind I wouldn't stay no longer."

"You made up your mind?" said Reeves. " 'Twas me told you to go."

"All right, have it your way," said Papa. "Anyhow I'm goin' where my young uns can git some education and learn to do a little figgerin'. I never went past the Fourth Grade myself. I reckon if I'd a stayed in school and learnt more about addin' up dollars and cents, I might a looked over them commissary books of yours and seen how you was robbin' and cheatin' me, and fixin' it so I couldn't never git a cent of cash money ahead but was always in debt at the end of the year. I'm goin' where my young uns can go to school instead of workin' all day in the cotton field, pickin' cotton." Papa looked over at Mama and smiled. "We'll git us a piece of land all our own. . . ."

"Fine!" sneered Reeves. "Where'll you git it—shiftless, lazy folks like you-all?" He climbed in his car and drove off.

They were all happy when he was gone. Papa took a paper bag from his pocket and passed it around. It was full of candy kisses wrapped in shiny paper. They each had one. Their cheeks bulged out fat as they sucked noisily.

"Whose car, Jim?" asked Mama.

They all looked at the old ramshackle Ford. It had a home-made two-wheeled trailer fastened on behind.

"Our'n," said Papa, with a sly smile. "It's gonna take us where we want to go. Come on, young uns, help me load up this plunder."

Papa and Joe Bob and Judy set to work. They put the larger pieces of furniture into the trailer and the bedsprings on top of the car. The oil stove and bundles of bedding were tied to the left runningboard, washtub and buckets on the spare tire in back.

"I got plumb sick of that ole mule and broke-down wagon your Uncle Barney gave us, Calla," said Papa. "Never could do no work with 'em nohow and had to use Reeves's all the time. So I swapped 'em for this-here jalopy. Hiram Adler's always ready to make a trade. You tell him what you got and he'll bid on it, no matter what it is—an ole sewing-machine——"

"Jim! You ain't traded off my sewin'-machine!"

"No, Calla, no, don't you worry. Or an ole iron bed——"

"Jim! You ain't traded off our iron bed?"

"No, Calla, no. Or a crop o' peanuts or watermelons half-ripe in the field or ary ole thing under the sun."

"Measly little ole crop o' peanuts this year," sniffed Judy. "Not worth the salt to bile 'em in." She put her hand in a small pail, took out a mouthful and began spitting out the shells.

"All right. Get in, everybody. We're off!" called Papa.

Mama picked up the carpet with roses on it. "Seems like I couldn't live without this carpet from my Mama's house," she said. She spread it over the front seat. Then she lifted in Cora Jane and the baby and climbed in herself.

"Oh, them molasses and the vittles," she called. "Judy, go bring 'em. We hid the molasses can when we saw Old Reeves a-comin'."

"But he couldn't take 'em," said Papa. "Them molasses is mine. Didn't I cook Roby Watson's syrup for him and take 'em for my pay?"

Judy brought the can and basket, and she and Joe Bob climbed into the crowded back seat. Papa started the engine and the car wheezed out the lane and off down the road. All the Drummonds, except the sleeping baby, looked back at the house that had been their home for three years. They didn't know whether to be glad or sorry. They were leaving the only home they had, but their hearts were high with hope.

Down at the bend in the road stood a group of colored people waiting—the Jenkins family. Judy looked at them. It was hard to think she might never play with Pinky and Daisy again, and that Joe Bob would forget the good times he had had with Porky and Arlie. Pinky came running up and thrust her greatest treasure—a little blue glass bottle—into Judy's hand. Judy leaned out of the car to call goodbye, and waved as long as she could see them.

"Wisht I could a seen Uncle Barney and Aunt Lissie once more," sighed Mama. Then she cheered up. "Tell us about the trade, Jim."

"Along with the mule an' wagon, I threw in the plow and shovels to boot," said Papa. "Hiram said he knew a man that wanted 'em. He said this ole jalopy was worth fifteen dollars anyhow. When I told him where I had in mind to go, he threw in the trailer free. Said he had no use for it. I told him I couldn't pay for it and he said to forget it. He's a good man, Hiram, and if ever I git ahead, I'll send him some money. This little ole Ford ain't much, but it goes if you give it oil and gas."

"Where we goin', Papa?" sang the children.

"We're leavin' Alabama for good," said Papa. "We'll git us a little piece o' land somewheres."

"Night's a-comin' on," said Mama. "We ain't had no supper but boiled peanuts. Where we gonna eat and sleep?"

"We'll camp out," said Papa. "We'll sleep out under the sky and count the stars."

"It's too cold," said Judy, shivering.

"I bought us some sliced baloney and a great big onion and two loaves of bread. . . ."

"Where *are* we goin', Jim?" asked Mama anxiously.

"Next best place to Heaven," sighed Papa happily. "Florida!"

"*Florida! Florida!*" echoed the children.

"Warm sun shines there all winter long and it don't never get cold at all," said Papa. "Man I met back in town was tellin' me about it. We'll set in the sun and when it gits too hot, we'll find us a palm tree and rest in the shade. Don't need no winter coats——"

"No? Honest to goodness? What'll we live on?" asked Mama.

"Cash money!" said Papa.

CHAPTER II

Florida

"You are my sunshine,
My only sunshine,
You make me happy
When skies are gray . . ."

OH, STOP your singin', Judy," said Joe Bob. "I'm tard of it."
Judy stopped singing abruptly and Papa began to talk.

"We'll jest go rollin' along without a care," said Papa. "We'll see the world, honey. We'll keep on goin' and never stop."

"We'll have to eat sometimes, Papa," said Judy.

"Shore, shore. Mama'll tell us when it's time to eat, and cook our meals. Mama's the best cook in the world—she can cook meals out of the air, right outa nothin'." Papa looked at Mama and smiled.

"What'll we git when we stop?" asked Judy.

"Ice cream and watermelon and honey in the comb, and biscuits and gravy . . ." laughed Papa.

Judy tucked her hand under her father's elbow and leaned back comfortably, with Cora Jane beside her. Mama and Lonnie and Joe Bob were in the back seat. Judy liked to dream as much as Papa did. The sky was bluer than any blue she had ever seen. It was as blue as the little blue glass bottle she held in her hand. She and Pinky had found it long ago in the cotton field and wondered how it got there. They took turns keeping it. Now Pinky wanted Judy to have it for good.

They drove for a long time through Alabama crop country, where the fields were bare and drab after the fall harvest. Now and then the level land was broken by tall woods along sluggish streams. Sometimes they stopped in towns and ate sandwiches or drank pop or ginger ale out of bottles. Then they went on again. Sometimes they passed a white-pillared mansion sitting back from the road under the shade of huge trees.

"Oh looky!" cried Judy. "What a pretty house. Wisht I could go inside. Betcha they got pretty carpet on all the floors. Was Grandma Wyatt's house like that?"

"No," said Mama. "Not big as that, but we had carpet."

They came to a county seat where a carnival was going on, so they stopped. The children took Papa's hand and walked around, looking at all the attractions. The carnival was noisy and Judy soon tired of it.

"I'll go back and take care of Lonnie," she said, "and let Mama come."

Making her way behind one of the tents, on a short cut to the Ford, she saw that the tent flap was lifted. Inside sat a very fat woman with black eyes and black hair braided in two long braids tied together at the end. She had few clothes on—only a skimpy bathing suit around her middle. At her feet stood a tin bucket of water. The woman was washing herself vigorously.

"Hello, dearie," she said. "Don't be scared, I won't hurt ye. I'm only havin' a bath. Never saw a fat lady take a bath before, did ye?"

Judy thought the woman must be cold, taking a bath outside in the wintertime. But she couldn't say a word.

"I'm Madame Rosie, the Fortune-Teller," said the woman. "See my sign out front? I used to travel with the circus, but now I follow these cheap little carnivals. Circus and carnival folks have to take their baths in buckets. They don't have no marble bathtubs, and no runnin' water, hot and cold, but they wash every day and they keep clean just the same." The woman laughed heartily. "A tin bucket's good enough for you and me, now ain't it, dearie? You wash one leg or one arm at a time, see?

"Now you just wait a minute." She disappeared behind a pink plush curtain. When she came out again, she was dressed in a flowered blouse and a bright blue velvet skirt.

"Come here, dearie, let me see your hand," she said. "I

charge fifty cents to read palms, but I know you ain't got a penny."

Judy stepped up obediently. Her hand was dirty and she thought the woman wanted to wash it clean. But she didn't. She turned it over and studied Judy's palm.

"You have a strong life-line," Madame Rosie said solemnly. "You'll live to be an old woman. There's a tall man with dark hair in your life . . . and hard work and grief and sorrow and dirt. . . ." She studied the girl's face. "You look like a little scared rabbit, but you got plenty of spunk. You've got a temper and a hot tongue and you often say things you're sorry for afterwards. *Better learn to hold your tongue* . . . think twice before you speak once . . . or you'll only make trouble for yourself. You carry a chip on your shoulder. Better shake it

off, stop being suspicious of people; be kind to them and you'll get along better. There's good in everybody." She looked at the girl's hand again. "I see a line of hope and beauty . . . a book with pictures in it . . . and a little white house set in a garden with a picket fence around it."

Madame Rosie let the girl's hand drop and turned away from her.

"Oh, I shouldn't have told her that," she said to herself. "It's there, but it can't be—the lines lie. She's dirt poor— never had a decent meal in her life. How could it come true? Why did I say it . . . puttin' impossible ideas in the poor child's head." She turned on the girl: "Have you lost your tongue? Why don't you say something? Go away—you little scared rabbit, you!"

Judy turned and went off through the high grass, stumbling over outstretched tent-ropes. She did not look back. She could not look back at the strange woman who had said such strange things and then said they could never come true.

Tears blinded her eyes until she could hardly see where she was going. Judy did not cry often. Life had always been hard and it did not seem to help any to cry about it. She climbed back into the car. She said nothing about Madame Rosie, but she was not to forget her for many a long day.

Mama didn't want to see the carnival after all. When Papa and the children came back, Papa said, "A man told me they've given up cotton round here and are growin' peanuts—peanuts and hogs."

"Let's stop here and make a crop o' peanuts, Jim," said Mama.

"No *ma'm*!" laughed Papa. "See that road sign down yonder? We're just eighteen miles from the Georgia and Florida lines. We're gittin' outa Alabama quick as we can."

It did not take them long. Entering Georgia, the first thing they noticed was the absence of cotton. Cotton fields gave place to pine woods and they passed several turpentine camps. Cows and hogs grazed on the grassy banks on both sides of the highway. A sign said: LOOK OUT FOR CATTLE AND HOGS. They saw a dead hog lying in the ditch.

"We better not drive too fast. We don't want to run over none of these-here Georgia critters," said Papa. "They might git the law on us."

They passed small villages of tiny Negro houses. At one country store, a large fish sawed out of wood was mounted on a post, and the sign said: FISH FOR SALE. Negro children played on porches or waded and fished in streams. Now and then they passed dark, dank cypress swamps where the Spanish moss hung in gloomy clusters and cypress knees poked up out of stagnant black water. This was Georgia.

Once they stopped at a small country store to get gas and water. A colored woman came up carrying a basketful of eggs.

"How much for your eggs?" asked Mama. But Papa shook his head.

"We must watch our pennies. Gotta have gas to take us where we're goin'."

[20]

"Goin' a long way?" asked the woman.

"To Florida," said Papa. "You live around here?"

"Yassir," said the woman. "Jest over yonder in that field a couple o' miles. Lawzy, my feetses hurts from walkin' so fur. Soon as I gits home I's gonna take off my shoes and rest my feetses good. Shoes is a heavy cross to bear."

The children had climbed out of the car to stretch. "You got shoes?" asked Joe Bob, wide-eyed. "Our'n wore out long time ago."

"Wisht I had *me* some shoes," said Judy softly.

She looked at the shoes on the woman's feet. They were men's old shoes, badly worn and broken out at the sides. But still they were shoes.

"You-all ain't got no shoes?" the woman asked. "And you

come from Alabam'? I went there oncet to visit my daughter and I like to froze to death. Slept under eight quilts, and one featherbed under and another'n on top. You shore need shoes to keep your feetses warm in Alabam'."

"Don't need none where we're goin'," laughed Papa. Then he added, "Nice country you got round here."

"No sir, 'tain't," said the woman. "This-here's bad country. Bad people live here. A man travelin' through here was robbed of all his money last week. Soon as I gits home I locks my door tight and takes off my shoes and rests my poor feetses."

"Know any place where we can camp for the night?" asked Papa.

"Five miles out is a creek," said the woman, going into the store. "But I tells you this is bad country, bad country."

They started on and came to the creek, but whether because of the robbers or not, Papa did not stop. When it was nearly dark, they turned off on a dirt side road.

"I'm tard," complained Cora Jane.

"Where do we sleep?" asked Joe Bob.

"We'll have us a picnic supper," said Papa, trying to be gay. "We'll camp out for the night and count the stars!"

Only Judy laughed. The others were too tired. Judy helped Papa rig up a shelter out of Mama's quilts against the side of the car. They ate their meager supper and stretched out on bedding spread on the ground. The ground was hard but they slept heavily.

In the middle of the night Joe Bob woke up. Out of the still-

ness came a weird cry: *A-whoo-a-whoo-a-whoo! A-whoo-a-
whoo-a-whoo!* He heard a rustling in the bushes.

"Papa!" shrieked the boy. "They're comin'—the bad men,
to rob you!"

Papa was awake at once. "How can they rob me, son, when
I got nothin' for 'em to take?"

Joe Bob could not stop crying. "Wisht I had my little ole
puppy dog to sleep with me," he sobbed.

"Cryin' won't bring him back, son," said Papa.

The next morning Papa got up early and disappeared. By
the time the others woke up, he was back with a large fish. He
built up a campfire and Mama fried fish and made hushpup-
pies out of corn meal. Breakfast tasted good and they forgot
the fears of the night before.

That day they passed many miles of pine forest and cypress
swamp. Even after they left Georgia and came into Florida,
there was little change in the landscape. Lonnie was fretful
and Mama had to fuss with him. She did not talk much, but
once she asked a question.

"Where we headin' for, Jim?"

"We'll go down through the center of the state—the lake
country," said Papa. "We might stop there if I can git me a
job in the citrus. Big orange country round them lakes. If not,
we'll go on down to South Florida where it's good and warm.
Feller I met back home told me there's money to be made down
there in beans, tomatoes and celery—cash money!"

"Cash money?" asked Mama, a little frightened at the sound

of the two words. It had been so long since she or Papa had seen more than a handful at cotton settling time.

"Yes *ma'm*!" said Papa.

"What doin'?" asked Mama.

"Pickin' beans," said Papa. "They grow more beans to the square inch down there than anywhere else in the U. S. A. Need thousands of pickers, the man said. Even young uns can pick."

"Oh Papa," said Judy, "can we help earn cash money?"

"I can pick beans," said Joe Bob. "I've picked cotton."

"I can pick too," said Cora Jane. "Faster'n you, Joe Bob."

"Well, me and Mama'll do the pickin'," said Papa, "and you-all can go to school every day. But that feller said that a man with his wife and a few young uns to help him could mop up a whole week's wages for one day's pick."

"They give a week's pay for one day?" asked Mama.

"Yes *ma'm*!" said Papa.

"But Jim, you said we was goin' where you could make a crop o' your own."

"We'll work in beans for a while if it brings in cash money," said Papa. "We'll save enough to make the down payment on a little farm of our own."

Papa liked to talk about Florida. "All them rich Yankee millionaires come down there and lie in the sun on Palm Beach and forget how cold it is up north. . . ."

"They have snow *up north,*" said Judy. "Did you ever see snow, Papa?"

[24]

"I'd like to see snow jest once," said Joe Bob. "Is it like cotton?"

"I never saw snow," said Papa. "Your Mama and me was born in Alabama and we never been up north where them Yankees live. Never wanted to go neither, 'cause one of them killed my Great-Grandpap long years ago in the War Between the States. They come down here, that Yankee army, and stole our crops and killed our men and freed the slaves and brung sorrow and destruction on us all. No-sir-ree, we-uns don't have no truck with them biggety Yankees, we don't."

"My Great-Grandma used to tell how hard they had it after that war," said Mama, "and how her and her young uns nigh starved to death."

"But I betcha snow is fun," said Joe Bob.

"It looks like sand, but it's cold as ice," said Judy. "Teacher told us that at school."

"We used to play like cotton was snow," said Joe Bob.

"Yes," added Judy, "you and me and Pinky and Daisy and Porky and Arlie—in the cotton field, instead o' pickin' cotton."

They laughed—but already it seemed a long time ago.

Papa was so busy dreaming about the future he didn't notice a lazy cow suddenly rise to her feet in the ditch and start to cross the road. The jalopy was bearing down hard before he saw her. He turned the wheel and swerved to the left to avoid hitting the animal, then turned quickly back into the road again.

"Danged ole critter!" exclaimed Papa. "Mighty close shave. We almost had roast beef for dinner that time!"

Cora Jane, standing in front of her mother's knees, was knocked against the windshield and began to cry lustily.

"Why didn't you bump her gentle-like and git us a cow?" asked Judy. "Got to have a cow on our farm, don't we?"

"Yes, but we don't want to pay damages and go to jail," laughed Papa.

"This-here one was a Florida cow," said Joe Bob. "She was skinnier than them Georgia critters."

"Not much difference that I can see," said Papa. "They leave 'em run in the woods to take care of themselves. Never feed 'em, and it don't look like there's much green grass for 'em to eat, pore things. That un we come nigh hittin' was so skinny, you could hang your hat on her hip-bone, it stuck out so fur."

Judy laughed. "Papa . . ." she began. "Papa . . ."

"What is it, sugarpie?" asked Papa.

"Thought you said it would be summer in Florida," Judy went on. "The grass ain't green nor nothin'."

"Just you wait, honey!" Papa promised. "Where we're goin', it'll be summer all year round."

Pine trees, their trunks close together like a million standing toothpicks, with palmetto thickets at their base, lined the roadside for hours. But at last there was a change. It was Judy who saw the first orange tree.

"Looky! Looky! Oranges growing on *trees*!" she cried.

"Mama, I want one to suck," said Joe Bob.

"Me too," said Cora Jane.

"What! You-all think it's settling time?" asked Judy.

Judy had not forgotten settlement time. The family always went to town when the cotton crop was sold. Even when the crop wasn't very good, it was a time to celebrate with something good to eat—maybe a few oranges to suck. When the crop was good and there was some cash money left over, it meant new clothes for everybody. Once, long ago, Mama got her sewing-machine and another time the iron bed—but Papa never got his new wagon. Judy remembered how few oranges there had been in the little house in the cotton field.

"Let's stop and pick and suck," begged Joe Bob.

Orange groves with their rich dark glistening leaves and golden balls of fruit lined the road now for miles, with the occasional break of a stretch of pine woods or a clear blue lake. The grass began to grow greener and the sky bluer. It began to feel more like summer. The children threw off their ragged coats and their bare legs were no longer cold.

All of a sudden the car began a queer knocking sound and Papa had to stop. He stopped by an orange grove and there on the ground lay ever so many good ripe oranges. While Papa got out his tools and fixed the engine and Mama tended Lonnie, the children ran into the grove and picked up oranges.

That night they had oranges for supper. The food they had brought from Alabama was all gone but a little flour and cornmeal. They sat on the grassy bank and sucked oranges—more

[27]

oranges than they had ever had in their lives before. Mama squeezed some juice in a cup and offered it to the baby. It was Lonnie's first taste—and he spat it out. He did not like it.

"Let's find us a lake to camp by," said Papa when the engine was fixed.

"A lake all our own," added Judy.

They left the main road and turned off on a network of sandy side roads. Papa always liked to explore. They passed farmhouses with wide verandahs and shade trees clustered close. The houses had house plants growing in large tin buckets on the verandahs, and one had a front yard full of blooming flowers.

"Looky!" cried Judy. "Flowers! It *is* summer! Summer in January!" She squeezed Papa's arm. "It's summer jest like you said it would be, Papa."

"Shore!" answered Papa, smiling.

CHAPTER III

The Little Lake

THE lake was beautiful. It was a perfect circle. The water was so clear and blue and glistening, they could see the fish swimming many feet below. All the Drummonds got out of the Ford and looked at it. All but Mama. She laid the sleeping Lonnie on the rose carpet on the front seat, took a carton from the back of the car and handed out soap.

"You're all as dirty as pigs," she said. "Git in that water and wash yourselves."

Judy remembered the muddy creek down below the cotton field where they used to wash in the summertime. Now they had a whole lakeful of clear, clean water and it was not cold at all.

Papa had driven the jalopy to the far side of the lake, and there in a clear place among the saw palmettos he had pitched camp. Scrub oaks grew on all sides and tall pines in the distance. "Nobody'll see us here so far from the road," Papa said. "We'll take our peace and rest a while."

The children paddled and splashed. Papa found the wreck of an old boat buried in weeds and grass at one side of the lake. He pulled it up on the bank and said he would fix it in the morning. Then all of a sudden, darkness fell and they hurried to bed.

"We'll go fishin', Papa," said Joe Bob the next morning.

"Bet your life we will," said Papa.

"All our vittles is gone, Jim," said Mama.

"We'll eat fish and I'll set a line for cooters," said Papa. "How about cooter turtle soup?"

Papa fixed up the holes in the boat, baited a line and strung it from one side of the lake to the other. The sun came out, pleasantly warm. Judy spread a quilt on the lake shore and Papa stretched out to rest. While the children splashed in the water and played with the boat, and Mama fussed with the clothes and supplies, Judy sat down beside Papa.

"Let's name it," she said. "We'll call it the 'Mirror of the Sky.' Down in the water you can see the white clouds and the blue sky and the trees and birds flying over. The lake is a looking-glass, and everything is upside down."

They propped their heads on their hands and looked down, then up.

"Mirror of the Sky—that's a nice idea, honey," said Papa.

Papa poked a crawling ant with a blade of grass and they

watched it for a long time. Mama came and sat down too and little Lonnie crawled on the quilt. He looked better and seemed more active.

"Nothin' like bein' outdoors," said Papa thoughtfully. "I'd hate to work all day long in a factory, sittin' by a roarin' machine and feedin' something into it, and rushin' and hustlin' to keep up with the blamed thing. Nothin' worse than bein' whistled in and whistled out. Machine's a big monster tryin' to gobble a feller up and break his spirit. Even when you're a sharecropper, you can be outdoors."

"But you can't call your soul your own," said Mama.

"There's no hope of gettin' ahead if a man can't be his own boss," Papa agreed. "Whatever happens, I'm proud I had the spunk to light out when I did."

"Whatever happens," said Mama, "we can't worst ourselves much."

"A little piece of land is all I want," Papa went on. "This is the only country in the world where all men are free and equal—that's what we stand for, anyway. The first settlers come here to git land, and for a long time everybody went west to git land. This country's always been a place where a man had the right to own a little piece of land."

"Maybe there ain't land enough to go round any more," said Mama. "So many big companies buyin' it up, a lone man ain't got a chance."

"There must be some places left. . . ." said Papa. "Well, look what's comin'—"

Several cows appeared, and soon the lake was surrounded by a large herd. The children took sticks and tried to chase them away.

"Woods cows," said Papa.

"Can we milk 'em and git us some milk?" asked Judy.

"Them skinny things?" laughed Papa. "Most of 'em's beef cattle, not milk cows, but don't give me a T-bone steak."

That afternoon the children took a long walk. A quarter of a mile away, they came to a large citrus grove. The trees were loaded with beautiful golden fruit and more fruit lay on the ground, starting to rot.

"We'll git us some oranges and tote 'em back," said Judy.

They began to pick them up. Suddenly, through the shadowy interior of the grove, they saw a man approaching. He

waved a stick and called out, but they could not hear what he said.

"Golly! It looks like Old Man Reeves," cried Judy, frightened. "We better run. But don't drop the oranges—it ain't stealin' when we take 'em off the ground."

The children ran as fast as they could.

"Will he catch us?" panted Joe Bob.

"And beat us?" cried Cora Jane.

"Keep running," called Judy.

The man did not follow, but turned around and went back.

"Papa, would he put us in jail for takin' oranges off the ground?" asked Cora Jane.

"Can't never tell," said Papa. "I don't know these-here Crackers or what they'd do."

That night the woods cows came again and the children chased them away. Mama made turtle soup for supper and they went to bed early. They hadn't been sleeping long when Joe Bob awoke, crying.

"There's somethin' in the bushes," he told Papa. "I heard it movin'—there it is. See?"

Papa saw two bright eyes shining straight at him from the darkness. He started after the animal with Mama's broom. Soon he came back and told Joe Bob to go to sleep again. But Papa did not close his own eyes all night.

The next morning when the children ran to play in the lake, they stopped suddenly on shore. A strange form was in the water, half-buried by grasses and weeds, not far from Papa's boat. It looked like a floating log—until it moved. Then it lifted its head and bellowed. It made a curiously hollow but powerful noise.

"Alligator! Alligator!" shrieked the children.

"An alligator in our lake," said Judy. "I never thought we'd git an alligator too."

"Likely he crawled overland from some pond or stream that dried up," said Papa. "Must be hungry, makin' such a noise."

"Can we feed him, Papa?" asked Joe Bob.

"He'd like a fat pig," said Papa, "if we had one. Likely he'll go off somewheres else and not bother us. I got to go to town soon, if I'm to get back before night. Want to go along?"

"What town, Papa?" asked Judy.

"Nearest one we can find," said Papa. "We'll go exploring."

Mama and the children stayed at the lake while Judy drove off in the car-and-trailer with her father. It took a good while to find a town, and still longer to find the store Papa wanted.

It was a funny store, with old stoves, beds and chairs standing on the sidewalk. The man, who had bushy hair all over his face, spent a long time looking over the furniture in the trailer. Was Papa swapping again? Judy knew how Papa loved to swap and she grew worried. She wanted to keep a few things for that farm they were going to get. She listened to the men's voices and when she heard the words *sewing-machine,* she jumped quickly out of the Ford.

The man and a boy helper were carrying Mama's bureau into his store.

"Papa! You're not swapping Mama's sewing-machine, are you?" She grabbed Papa's arm and shook it. "Papa! Listen to me!" She stamped her foot but Papa turned away.

"Papa! If you swap Mama's sewing-machine . . ."

"Git back in the car and stay there!" said Papa angrily.

Papa almost never spoke a cross word to Judy. But she did not care how mad he got. She gritted her teeth and clenched her fists. She'd fight him if he swapped Mama's sewing-machine.

"Papa . . . Papa . . ."

"Git back in that car and stay there!" repeated Papa.

Slowly Judy climbed back into her seat. She watched out

the back car window and saw the table go into the second-hand store, but not the sewing-machine. She felt better. She saw the man bring out a large bulky bundle of heavy canvas and put it on top of the trailer. What was Papa getting?

He didn't explain when he came back to his seat. He didn't say a word. But Judy guessed he must have gotten some money to boot, because he stopped at a store and came out with two large paper bags full of groceries. He was smiling.

"Now we'll eat again, honey," he said. "I got us some flour and meal and fatback and saleratus and coffee and black-eyed peas. Here's a dime for you. Want to go in the store and git some candy?"

Judy looked at the dime. She closed her fist over it tightly. "No," she said. "I'll keep it—a while anyway."

Papa started the jalopy, and on the edge of town they passed a big barn with a sign that said: G. A. PRATT—STABLES. All the cars and trucks and wagons on the road seemed to be turning in at the gate.

"Wonder what's goin' on," said Papa. "Let's go see."

Judy smiled. Papa was always ready to do the unexpected. He went in to look around and soon came out again.

"Come on, git out," he said. "It's as good as a circus. They're auctionin' off livestock in there and farmers from all over the county are biddin'. Likely we could git us that cow you said we'd ought to have on our farm."

Judy climbed down. "But how can you pay for a cow,

Papa, without cash money? Don't we have to pay for the farm first?"

"Shore do," said Papa. "But let's go in—this is free."

They walked through the barn to the "auction ring" at the back. Rows of seats were built up on three sides for a grandstand. The place was crowded, but they managed to slip into the second row from the front.

The auctioneer sat in an elevated box on one side, and chanted in a swift jabber-jabber-jabber as he accepted bids from men in the audience. A Cracker boy, wearing overalls and a black felt cowboy hat, rode a spotted cattle pony into the ring and out again. Bidding was swift; farm animals one after the other were sold and let out of the ring.

When the first cow was brought in, Judy held her breath, for fear Papa might buy it. If so, how would he pay for it? All the buyers paid cash before they took their animals away. The cow was dirty white, thin and scrawny. Other cows were brought in, one after the other. Each time, Judy looked up at Papa but he shook his head.

"Don't worry, sugar," he said. "We want a better cow than that."

Then came the mules, and after the mules, pigs and hogs. A peanut man, wearing a white apron, stepped about on the grandstand, calling, "Peanuts! Buy peanuts!" Papa bought a bag, and he and Judy began to munch.

After the pigs had all been sold, a goat was brought in— a white, hornless Nanny goat. At the gate she balked. The

Cracker boy pulled on the rope with all his might. Then suddenly the goat stopped balking and rushed forward across the ring. The boy fell over backwards and the crowd yelled.

"I told you it was good as a circus!" laughed Papa.

The boy had a hard time managing the goat, because the goat didn't like the boy and kept rushing at him with her head lowered. The people kept on laughing and the auctioneer couldn't start the bidding.

At last the goat backed off into a corner and waited there, eyeing the crowd and shaking her head. The auctioneer did his best, but nobody would bid.

"Won't somebody start this good milk-goat off at a quarter?" begged the man. "We got to start somewhere. Mighty good milker—it would take six men and a boy to do it!"

"The critter's lame," said a farmer. "Her ole man kicked her—good reason too."

"A quarter—gimme a bid of a quarter," begged the auctioneer. "I got to sell her . . . a quarter, have I got a quarter?"

Judy breathed hard and glanced swiftly down at the coin in her hand. Then suddenly she called out in a high shrill treble: "Ten cents! I'll give you a dime!"

Everybody looked at her and laughed. Her face turned pink as she hid it against Papa's shirt sleeve.

"Did I hear a dime—ten cents—from that little gal down there in the second row?" asked the auctioneer.

"You shore did!" answered Papa.

"Sold!" said the auctioneer. "This-here gal young un has

bought that mean ole goat." He turned to Judy. "She's your'n. You ain't afraid of her? Bring your money up here and take your goat away. We don't never want to see her again."

Judy hopped over the bench in front, handed her dime up to the desk and approached the goat.

"Better be keerful," warned the black-hatted boy. "She'll butt you all over the place. She's MEAN."

"I'm not afraid," said Judy.

The people held their breath as they watched. A woman cried, "Don't let her!" Another said, "Why don't her Pa take the goat?"

Judy patted the animal on the head and said in a low voice: "I never thought I'd git a goat." She picked up the rope and the goat followed her, limping meekly out of the ring. Papa walked behind while all the people clapped.

When they got back to the car, Judy said: "Was it all right for me to buy a goat instead of candy, Papa?"

"Shore," said Papa, smiling. "It was your dime and you got a bargain. A good milk goat's worth five or six dollars. But do you reckon you'll like it as well as candy?"

Judy grinned. "Dunno," she said. "It depends on how she behaves. She's an old mischief, I can see that. 'Mischief'— that's what I'll name her. 'Mischief' and 'Missy' for short."

Papa moved the canvas aside and they put Missy in the trailer, tying her up well with the rope. When they reached the little lake, there were two surprises—the goat and the second-hand tent. Papa put the tent up right away, and explained it wasn't safe for them to sleep in the open as they had been doing, because of alligators, possible bob-cats and other night prowlers. Then they looked at the goat.

"Gonna feed her to the 'gator?" asked Joe Bob.

"Mercy, no," said Mama. "She'll give you young uns milk to drink, if we can find anything to feed her."

"Save up your tin cans!" laughed Papa.

"She can ride in the trailer," said Mama. "Leave her there tonight so that ole 'gator won't bother her." Mama didn't say a word about the table and bureau being gone.

That night Papa fastened the tent up tight and neither the cows nor the alligator came to disturb the Drummond family. He got up early the next morning and took a swim in the lake. He was partly dressed when suddenly, beyond a clump of palmettos, appeared a man on horseback. The man came close to the tent and pulled up. Mama and the children came out and stared.

"What you folks doin' *here*?" the man demanded. He got down from his horse.

"Campin'," said Papa, pulling up his overalls.

"You better get out and get out quick," said the man in a low voice.

"Get out—why?" asked Papa.

"You got no right to camp here," growled the man.

"No?" said Papa. "It's a free country, ain't it?"

Joe Bob whispered to Judy, "Looks like Old Man Reeves."

"It's the same man we saw in the orange grove," said Judy.

[42]

Perhaps the man heard her, for he said promptly, "I saw them kids o' your'n stealin' oranges in my grove yesterday. They run like rabbits when I called. Don't you know I can arrest 'em for pickin' an orange?"

Judy stepped forward. "Didn't pick none," she said. "Your oranges was jest a rottin' on the ground, mister. *You* didn't want 'em. Why couldn't we have some to eat?"

Judy and Joe Bob disappeared back of the trailer.

"I'll have the law on you folks," the man went on. "Good thing I was out ridin' in the woods lookin' to see how many new calves my cows had dropped."

"Them your cattle roamin' through here?" asked Papa.

"Shore," said the man.

"This your land here, and your lake?"

"No," said the man. "My place is over beyond my orange grove, quarter mile down that road."

"This is not your land, and you're orderin' us off?" asked Papa. "What your cows doin' here?"

"Grazin'," said the man. "They go where they want to. It's Open Range in this county. You folks better git out or I'll . . ."

The man did not finish his sentence because a limping goat rushed suddenly out from behind the trailer, rammed her hard head into his knees and knocked him over. The man yelled and swore at the top of his voice.

"Missy! Missy! Come here!" called Judy, running out and trying to grab the goat's rope. "She got loose, Papa, I couldn't

[43]

help it." Joe Bob was peeping from behind the trailer, giggling.

"I'll . . . I'll have the law on you folks!" sputtered the grove man, getting to his feet and dusting himself off. "Assault—stealin' fruit—campin' unlawful . . ."

Papa stepped up close as the man mounted his horse to go.

"Let me get this straight," he said. "The cattle are allowed to come here by this lake, but people are not. Is that it?"

"You said it!" answered the man.

As soon as he was gone, Papa turned to Mama and said, "Pack up as quick as you can. We're gettin' out."

A half-hour later a rickety jalopy with a trailer behind moved out of the palmettos beside the little lake and took to the road, traveling southward.

CHAPTER IV

The Middle-Sized Lake

"ME—EH! Me—eh!" bleated Missy in the trailer.

"We must stop at a feed store and get some grain to feed that goat," said Mama. "We must milk her too."

"If she'll let us," said Joe Bob.

"Course she'll let us milk her," said Judy.

They had been riding most of the day, through many towns and past many lakes and orange groves. Palm trees, pine trees, even orange trees were so common now Judy did not notice them. It seemed a long time since the Drummonds had left Alabama, and every turn of the jalopy's wheels seemed to make life in the cotton field fade farther away into the past.

"There's a feed store," said Joe Bob, pointing.

Papa pulled up and gave Judy a quarter. She jumped out

of the car and mounted the platform. Large sacks of feed and fertilizer were piled up inside the wide-open doors, and several men were hauling sacks on small hand trucks.

Judy looked about her. The place was dusty and had a strong fertilizer smell. She stared at the pile of feed sacks. The sacks were made of printed cotton cloth, flowered designs of pink or blue on a white ground. Judy tried to decide which pattern she liked best.

"Whatcher want, kid?"

The man who came up was fearful to look at. Judy shuddered. He had one eye shut and one eye open. His hair was red, and he had few teeth inside his big mouth. His overalls were white with dust.

"Me—eh! Me—eh!" Judy could hear Missy bleating. She

glanced across the street. There on the sidewalk, Papa was down on his knees trying to milk the goat, while Joe Bob was hanging on to her rope for dear life.

"Some cow-chop . . . for the goat . . ." stammered Judy. She looked at Missy instead of the man. "I only got a quarter—"

"That your goat?" grinned the man. "Good at buttin', eh?" He walked away. Somebody called him: "Hey, Charlie, One-Eyed Charlie!" He came back after a while with some grain in a paper bag. "Real goat-chop," he said, "better'n cow-chop."

Judy got up her courage and pointed to the flowered sacks. "What do you do with 'em when you empty 'em?" she asked.

"We sell the grain to the farmers," said One-Eyed Charlie. "Their women-folks make purty dresses outa the sacks. One sack makes a dress for a gal big as you."

"Shore 'nough?" gasped Judy.

"Yes *ma'm!*" grinned the man.

"Could I . . . could I?"

"Next time you come round, I'll have one of them sacks for you," said One-Eyed Charlie. "What color you like best?"

"Blue," said Judy. "You . . . you'll give me one?"

"Shore will," grinned the man.

He was kind, after all, in spite of his fearful appearance. You never could tell by people's looks what they were like underneath.

"Me—eh! Me—eh!" bleated Missy across the street.

"Your goat's callin' you!" The man laughed.

Judy ran. Only when Missy put her nose down into the goat-chop did she consent to stand still enough to be milked. And Judy was the only one who could milk her.

Papa drove right on again. When they were five miles beyond the town, Judy suddenly remembered. "Oh Papa . . ." she began.

"What is it, sugarpie?"

"One-Eyed Charlie said . . . if I'd come back . . . he'd give me——"

"Who on earth is One-Eyed Charlie?" asked Papa.

"The man in the feed store," said Judy. "He promised me a blue flowered feed sack next time I come in, and now *we won't never go there no more.* . . ."

"What you want a feed sack for?" asked Papa gently.

"To make a dress," said Judy. "Mama could sew it on her sewing-machine . . ."

"You ain't got dresses?" Papa looked down at her faded and torn overalls, as if noticing them for the first time.

"Only two," said Judy, "and one is tore and patched. The others got too small. Cora Jane's wearin' 'em."

"Too bad," said Papa, "but there's other feed stores and Missy will be needin' more grain, won't she?"

Judy nodded. They went riding on.

"I like the prosperous look of this citrus country," said Papa. "We'll stop by this-here lake and have swims before we go to bed. It's bigger'n that other lake of our'n—sort of middle-sized, I reckon. All these towns seem to be full of lakes. Lakeland has fourteen, Orlando twenty-five. Likely I can get me a job in this purty little town."

Papa picked out a place to camp between the lake and the road. But first he inquired where the owner of the land lived and went to ask his permission. The owner said, "Go ahead!" and gave Papa a bagful of tangerines for the children.

Papa put up the tent and unloaded the kerosene stove. Mama cooked a big meal—fried meat, grits and gravy and molasses. While they were standing around eating, they noticed that people passing in cars were staring at them. Mama did not like it.

"We'd ought to stopped on a back road, Jim," she said.

"They can look at us," Papa said, "but they can't run us off this time."

After supper Papa walked back into the town to inquire about getting a job in citrus. He hadn't been gone long when a car stopped by the tent and a man got out.

"I am Captain Pendleton, of the Salvation Army," he told Mama. "I came out to see if I could help you."

"Help me?" gasped Mama. "Help me what?"

"Well . . . several people notified me they had seen a family with young children campin' by Lake Packer . . ." said Captain Pendleton awkwardly, "and my organization is always ready to lend a helping hand to those in . . . er . . . need. You don't intend to sleep here, do you?"

"Shore do," said Mama. "That's what we put our tent up for."

"But it's too cold for little children to sleep on the ground,"

[49]

said the captain. "Now we have good, clean beds at our Shelter in town . . ."

"Why, this ain't cold!" spoke up Judy. "You'd jest ought to spend a winter in Alabama in a little ole piecy house with the wind blowin' the covers right offen the beds!"

"We been sleepin' on the ground ever since we left home," said Joe Bob.

"We got a mattress," said Mama proudly. "We make pallet beds out of quilts for the young uns."

"On the *ground*?" asked the captain, shocked.

"Shore," said Mama. "When we stop for one night, we don't trouble to set up the iron bed."

"We been havin' a cold spell," said the captain. "Hit went clear down to 40° the other night, and the paper says hit might freeze tonight."

"Huh!" sniffed Mama. "It's a heap colder'n that where we come from. This feels warm to us."

"We always aim to help the destitute," said the captain lamely.

"We ain't destitute," said Mama.

"We got a goat," said Joe Bob.

"Me—eh! Me—eh!" bleated Missy.

The captain gave up and went away.

Then a newspaper reporter came. He took a large camera out of his car, set it up on a tripod and pointed it at the tent.

"What you want?" demanded Mama.

The children stood and stared. Judy held Lonnie who began to cry.

"Stand still just as you are," said the man. "I'll take your picture before it gets too dark and then I'd like to get your story. It's for the local paper. I'm a reporter." He worked fast and before they knew it, had snapped the picture.

"What story?" asked Mama.

"Oh, just who you are and where you came from, and how many children you got, and what you're doing here, and where you're going," said the man. Briskly he got out his notebook and pencil. "Captain Pendleton's been to see you, hasn't he?"

Mama hesitated. She didn't know what to do or say. "Judy," she called. "Look see, is Papa comin'?"

"No, I don't see him, Mama," said Judy. "Here, you take Lonnie and put him to bed. I'll talk to this feller. You jest leave him to me."

"Now, be mannerly," said Mama. "Don't say nothin' to rile him."

Mama went into the tent. Judy stepped up to the man, her arms akimbo, her bright eyes flashing.

"You're outa your place, mister, a-runnin' round here takin' pictures of people who all they want is to be let alone. We ain't hurtin' nobody and we never said we wanted to have our picture in the paper, 'cause we don't."

"Not if it helped your father to get a job and a house to live in?" asked the reporter.

Joe Bob stepped up. "I'd jest like to cut that thing to pieces —that thing you take pictures with. If I jest had a knife, I'd . . ."

The man folded up his tripod hastily.

"What you takin' our pictures for?" demanded Judy. "We ain't done nothin' wrong. You'll be tryin' to put us in jail next. Well, my Papa *asked* if we could camp here and the man said yes!"

Without a backward glance, the reporter climbed into his car and drove off. He hadn't been gone long before a large shiny black car pulled up and two well-dressed, middle-aged ladies stepped out.

"We're from the Women's Philanthropic Welfare Circle," they said.

Mama came out of the tent and frowned.

"Oh, how cold you poor people must be, camping in this damp place on a cold night like this," said the first lady.

"No, we ain't cold," Mama said patiently. "This seems warm to us."

The women stared at Judy and the children. "At least your children might put on their shoes and stockings. Their legs look blue," said the second lady.

"Ain't got no shoes," said Joe Bob.

"Ain't got no stockin's," said Judy.

"How long since they've had a bath?" asked the first lady.

Mama turned her back and did not answer.

"I will be glad to let you and your children sleep on my back porch, if you'll come home with me," said the second lady. "You can all have nice warm baths in the bathroom first. Just how many are there of you? You folks always have such big families."

"We don't like baths," said Joe Bob.

"We like to be dirty," said Judy.

"We like to play in the dirt," said Cora Jane.

It was fun to be obstinate. All the children's impudence was coming out—they were trying to make their unwelcome visitors go away. Mama heard Lonnie cry and brought him out of the tent in her arms.

"And that's your poor baby," said the first lady. "He's sickly, isn't he?"

"No, jest ornery," said Mama.

"And your poor husband has no job?" asked the second lady.

"He's gone to see about gittin' one," said Mama.

"You won't come home with me then?"

"Can't leave all our plunder here by the lake and be gone when the old man gits back," said Mama patiently.

"How long since you've had a good meal?" asked the first lady.

"Half an hour," said Mama.

Judy could stand it no longer. Mama was tired and the women were pestering her to death. She walked boldly up —as boldly as if she were facing Old Man Reeves himself, and spoke loudly: "Why can't you-all go away and leave us alone?"

But the ladies, intent upon doing good, ignored her. "I'll get your husband a job in one of the citrus plants in the morning," the second lady said.

"And I know where there's a nice little house for you to live in," said the other.

"Don't want your nice little ole . . ." began Judy, but she stopped suddenly. They *did* want a house and a home and a job for Papa. They wanted it more than anything in the world. Judy was stricken with regret that she had been rude to the ladies. She bit her tongue. That fortune-teller was right—her hot tongue was always getting her into trouble. Then she listened to what Mama was saying. Mama was always patient. Mama never lost her temper. First she had been annoyed by that captain and than by that reporter and now by these prying women, but Mama never said a rude word.

"Jim won't take a job inside," Mama was saying quietly. "He can't stand it to be cooped up indoors. Can he git a job pickin' oranges?"

"No," said the lady, "that's done by colored men—experienced pickers, trained for the work. Of course if your husband is a good grove man——"

"What's that?" asked Mama.

"A man who knows all about growing oranges and grapefruit and work on a grove."

"Jim never saw an orange tree in his life until three days

ago," said Mama. "He was born and bred in an Alabama cotton field."

"Too bad," said the lady. "Too bad we can't help you."

"We don't need help," said Mama. "We'll make out. We always have."

The ladies went to their car, shaking their heads. Their words floated back: "You try to give them food and shelter, and a good steady job, but they refuse it all. They *like* to live like that, unwashed, improperly fed." As they drove off, one lady leaned her head out and called cheerfully, "We'll be back to see you in the morning. We'll bring you some clean clothes and a basket of groceries."

It got dark and Mama and the children went inside the tent. When Papa returned from town, they were all awake, sitting in the darkness, waiting for him.

"Did you get you a job?" asked Mama.

"No," said Papa. "The plants were all closed, but I talked to some men about it. The trouble about citrus is this—you got to work in the packing plant, 'cause all the outside work, pickin' the fruit and takin' care of the trees, is done by colored men. I don't think I want to start workin' indoors in nice weather like this."

"Just what I told them ladies," said Mama.

"What ladies?"

Then the story of the unwelcome visitors came out.

"Puttin' our picture in the paper!" Papa was mad. "I'd like to put a stop to that. Campin' on the highway ain't so good, even if we did git permission. People botherin' their heads about us is worse than bein' ordered off the place. We go from the fryin' pan into the fire, don't we?"

"They mean well, I reckon," said Mama.

"Papa, one lady said she had a little house for us to live in," said Judy wistfully.

"We don't want her little ole house," said Papa.

"But the jalopy might break down and we couldn't go no farther," said Joe Bob.

"Don't worry, son, I can fix it," said Papa.

"If the lady gits you a job, Papa, we won't always have to be drivin' to a new place," said Judy.

"Gittin' tard o' travelin', honey?" asked Papa. "I thought you liked to go rollin' along."

"I'm dog-tard of it," said Judy.

"So are we all," said Papa, "but we got a little farther to go . . . We ain't got to Heaven yet, have we, Calla?"

Mama shook her head and hushed Lonnie.

"They're comin' back first thing in the mornin' and bringin' us clothes and vittles in a basket," sang out Joe Bob. "I heard 'em say so."

"Do you reckon they'll bring shoes and stockin's?" asked Judy, her eyes aglow with eagerness.

If only she could get a pair of shoes, she would be willing to do without the stockings. A pair of shoes—any size, whether they fitted her or not. *Oh, if I'd a been nice to them ladies, they mighta brought me stockin's too. But I was mean. I said*

*mean things. But likely they'll bring shoes and stockin's any-
way——*

"Go to bed and get to sleep," said Papa. "We'll make a
soon start in the mornin'."

"You'll wait till them ladies come back, won't you, Papa?"
cried Judy. In her voice was all the longing she felt.

"What for, honey?"

Judy couldn't say out loud what she was thinking. Papa
wouldn't understand. He didn't know how badly she wanted
shoes, and she couldn't find the words to tell him.

"You done right to say we're not destitute, Calla," said
Papa. "Why, we're *rich*! We're not exactly loaded down with
this world's goods, but we got each other, and we got four
nice kids, and we ain't never starved yet. We're not destitute,
and we don't take *charity* off nobody. We still got our pride."

The next morning at daybreak, the tent came down and the
jalopy drove off with the trailer behind it. Not a trace of the
last night's camping except broken-down grasses could be
seen when a large shiny black car pulled up and stopped later
in the day.

"They're gone," said a lady inside the car. "What did I
tell you?"

"Thankless ingratitude," said her companion.

*   *   *

Papa stopped at a filling station and talked for a long time
to some men there. When he came back to the car, he had a
new map and he pointed out the route the man had showed

him. Judy read off the names of the towns: Lake Wales, Frost-proof, Avon Park, Sebring, Childs, Hicoria and Moore Haven.

"Oh, see all the lakes on the map!" cried Judy. "This one, where we're goin', is the biggest of all. O—kee—cho—bee! What a funny name."

"Indian name for 'big water,' the man told me," said Papa. "Advised me to go down around the southeast corner of the lake, near Belle Glade. He said a family can make twenty to thirty dollars a week in beans."

"What kind o' work?" asked Mama.

"Gradin' beans," said Papa. "It's light work that women folks can do—just watchin' the stuff go by on the belt and pickin' out the culls."

"Go by on a belt? What you mean, Papa?" asked Judy.

"It's in a packing house, where they pack beans and green stuff to ship up north," explained Papa. "There's machinery that keeps a wide belt movin', and the beans come along on the belt, and you pick out the bad ones and toss 'em in a basket. That's all there is to it."

"Sounds easy," said Mama. "But will you like workin' in-doors, Jim?"

"I can stand it for a while, jest to make a little cash money," said Papa thoughtfully.

It was dark by the time they reached Moore Haven, and everybody was tired and sleepy, so Papa lost no time making camp in a vacant lot on the edge of town. Soon the Drummonds were all fast asleep.

CHAPTER V

The Big Lake

THEY drove over from Moore Haven the next morning. The road was filled with cars, trucks and trailers, many of them loaded down and piled high with furniture.

"Where's everybody goin'?" asked Mama.

"To Bean Town, I reckon," said Papa. "All the people in them cars will be lookin' for jobs in beans, like me."

They stopped at a garage to have air put in the tires. "This Bean Town?" Papa asked.

"Shore is," said the garage man, who had a nice face and a friendly smile. "All round here is beans and up the east shore of the lake too. Black muck soil ten to twenty feet deep. We shore can grow string beans, cabbage and other garden truck. We send all the stuff *up north* for them Yankees to eat. Where you folks from?"

"Alabama," said Papa.

"Some come from clear across the continent. We've got people from every state in the Union right here. Looks like you've come to stay!" laughed the man.

"Can I git me a job?" asked Papa.

"Shore can," replied the man. "They couldn't harvest that bean crop without you. You can get a job here if you can anywhere."

The cheerful way the man talked made Papa feel good. "Ary place to live in this-here town?" he inquired.

"What you want?" asked the man. "House? Hotel room? Boarding house? Tourist cabin? The town's crowded—all full up. There hasn't been an empty room since last November —all grabbed up quick before the fall crops began. Of course some growers have houses or barracks for their own workers to live in, and over to Belle Glade, the government's put up a camp for white people. Camp Osceola they call it, but I hear they're turnin' folks away every day. Hit's plumb full."

Papa looked disappointed. "Just what would you advise?"

"Well, you migrants will have to find your own housing," said the man. "That's the only way."

"What's that you're callin' us?"

" 'Mi-grants'—hit means people that migrate, follow the season, on the go all the time. Migratory people—like migratory birds, you know."

"Never heard of 'em," said Papa.

"Never heard o' them bluebirds and redbirds and robins that go up north in summer and come south in winter?" laughed the man.

"Oh, shore!" said Papa. "Migratory! Mi-grants! So that's us, on the go all the time. What did you say we should do?"

"You'll have to git your own quarters," said the man, "and don't expect nothing fancy. I tell you what you do—go down to the next corner, turn right and keep going till you get out on the south side of town. There's a drainage canal there, and a bunch o' white folks—migrants like you—livin' on the bank. They'll help you get fixed up."

Papa thanked the man and followed his directions.

The town was full of large warehouses and loading platforms. Along the main streets were two-story business buildings, restaurants, general stores and recreation places. Then came residences, boarding houses and good and bad cottages of every description. At last they found the drainage canal.

It was like a little town in itself, all stretched in a line on the high canal bank. The houses were jammed close together, and they were all kinds—tents, trailers, tar-paper shacks, hovels of galvanized tin, and packing-box houses—all out in the bright, broiling sun. The only shade came from scattered clumps of banana trees and rank-growing castor-bean plants.

Papa got permission to camp on the canal bank at a dollar a week ground rent. He found an empty place between two other shacks, where he set up the tent and unpacked the trailer. Then he went off to town to inquire about a job.

"Not much green stuff for Missy to eat," said Judy, unloading the goat and staking her on the slope. She looked at the water hyacinths and cattails choking the canal.

"Good place to fish," said Joe Bob. He lost no time in rigging up a fish line and digging worms for bait.

"Oh, you got a sewing-machine!" said a strange voice. A woman put her head out of a small window in the tar-paper shack next door. "Where you folks from anyway?"

"Alabama," said Judy. Mama came out of the tent.

"My name's Harmon, Edie Harmon," said the neighbor.

"I'm Calla Drummond," said Mama, and she told her children's names.

"We're from California and from Michigan before that," laughed Mrs. Harmon. "But they're all alike—these dumps. After a while you get so you don't feel you're human any more. You get so dirty——"

"Where's the water?" asked Mama.

Mrs. Harmon pointed. "Down in the canal—it's water drained off from the lake."

"You use that to wash with?" asked Mama.

"Sure, and to drink too."

"That dirty water?"

"Drinkin' canal water hasn't killed nobody yet that I know of," said Mrs. Harmon. "I was squeamish, too, just like you, when I first started out. But after a while you get used to it and it ain't so bad. The kids like it—my kids has a mighty good time here. There's rabbits to run and plenty o' catfish in the canals, and there's always dried beans to scrape out from under the plants if you know what fields ain't been picked over but once or twice."

"Here, Judy," called Mama. "Go down and dip us up some o' that water."

"My land! I'm sure glad you got a sewin'-machine," said Mrs. Harmon. "I been needin' to mend my old man's overalls for a long time, and I can do it so much faster on the machine. You folks'll like it here."

Judy took the water bucket and went down the canal bank to fill it. It was good to get out of the sound of the woman's voice. She sat down and sunk her head in her hands.

It wasn't what she had been expecting at all. There was no farm, no house, no yard with a fence.

There was only the second-hand tent they had camped in on the trip. The tent was their home, and they were still camping out. The farm and the house and yard were fading away into the dim and unknown future, just as the house in the cotton field had faded away into the past.

The tent and the canal bank and the canal—these were real. This was the present. This was all they had.

"*Ju-dy! Ju-dy!*" Suddenly she heard Mama calling. She dipped the bucket down among the cattails and brought it up full of water. She hurried up the bank.

"Don't know why you have to take all day," said Mama.

Mrs. Harmon had come over and brought her own rocking-chair. She sat talking with Mama as if they had always known each other. She was holding Lonnie on her lap.

"I thought there was a lake," said Judy, "the biggest lake in Florida, Okeechobee. Where's the lake, Miz Harmon?"

"Right over beyond Bean Town," replied the woman, "but you don't never see it. It's on the other side of the dike, and the dike's forty feet high, I guess. You got to look up at it and then there's nothing to see. They built the dike after that big hurricane in 1928."

"What's a dike?" asked Judy.

"A big pile o' gravel to hold the water back—about two hundred feet wide at the bottom and thirty feet wide on top.

It goes around the south and east sides of the lake, to stop the floods. When a hurricane comes, it can blow so strong across the lake, it makes a regular tidal wave and splashes right over on all sides. But that don't happen often, of course."

"You been comin' here long?" asked Mama.

"This is our third winter," said Mrs. Harmon. "We like Florida for winters, even if it don't pay so good. We go back to Michigan summers. I like Florida, I like to sit in the sun."

"You don't work?"

"Yes, we all work, my big kids and my husband and me, when the packin' plants git goin'. There's only one opened up so far. I sit in the sun till the rush season starts. My youngest is a girl, Bessie—she's twelve and in school."

"In school?" asked Judy. "Where's a school?"

"Over on the other side of town," said the woman.

"Oh Mama, can I go?" begged Judy.

"Bessie will take you," said Mrs. Harmon. "The school would be jammed if all the workers' kids went. But most of the migrants don't bother to send 'em, they're here for such a short time anyway."

"Oh Mama, can me and Joe Bob and Cora Jane go?" asked Judy.

"We'll have to ask Papa," said Mama.

Papa looked pretty blue when he came back from town. He was no longer gay and happy as he had been on the trip. Judy decided not to mention school.

"The packing houses where you make all that cash money

ain't open yet," he said. "It's been cold and the beans been held back. They're not ready for picking."

"No other crops ready?" asked Mama.

"No, beans will be first. They use Negroes outside and whites inside," said Papa. "The colored folks do all the picking. There's a big colored quarter in town and several camps for them. Cars are bringin' 'em in from every direction."

"What'll we do?" asked Mama. "Move on again?"

"No, I reckon we better stay right here till beans come in," said Papa. "Likely I can find a small grower to give me day work." He turned to Judy. "They got a nice school, honey."

"Miz Harmon told us," answered Judy. "Said Bessie would take me. Can I go?"

"Shore can," said Papa. "My young uns ain't goin' to work in beans. They're goin' to school to learn a few things."

Mama got ready to do a big washing. Judy carried water to fill the washtub and Joe Bob found scraps of kindling and built a fire under it. When all the clothes were washed, Mama spread them out on the canal bank to dry.

Nobody knew how Missy got loose, but she did.

Judy came out of the tent and found her there, chewing on Papa's overalls. Other clothes were torn into shreds and scattered about. Missy was taking a taste of everything. Judy stared at the sight.

" 'Mischief' is your name for shore," she said. She grabbed a stick from the pile by the tub, went after the goat, and whacked her soundly on the back. After a few blows, Missy turned her head and gave one look at the girl with her sad eyes. Judy dropped the stick and put her arms around the goat's neck.

"Oh, did I hurt you?" she cried. "You've had no goat-chop to eat, that's why you ate our clothes. You're hungry . . . I must find a feed store." She took the goat farther down the canal and staked her.

One of Judy's dresses was ruined, the other, the patched one, still held together. She spread it out carefully, trying to smooth the wrinkles. There was no iron to iron it, but at least it was clean.

"Hey, Judy! You ready?" sang out Bessie Harmon next morning.

"Shore am," answered Judy. Judy was to go alone the first day, without Joe Bob and Cora Jane, to see what the school was like.

Bessie Harmon was a large girl with plain features and straight hair worn in two braids. She had a blunt, rough way of talking and Judy did not know what to make of her.

"Ain't you even combed your hair?" she demanded.

"I . . . we . . . we lost the comb . . ." stammered Judy.

Bessie jerked her by the arm. "Wait here." She disappeared inside the tar-paper shack and came out with a comb. She dipped it into water in a basin on the bench and combed Judy's hair. She kept on wetting and wetting the comb until Judy's hair was plastered down flat. "Don't you ever braid it or curl it or do somethin' with it?"

"No," said Judy. "I just leave it be."

"You gotta comb your hair every day before you go to school," scolded Bessie. "Did you wash your face? Our teacher won't take dirty kids in her class. She sends 'em home to wash up."

"I took a bath," said Judy. "I'm clean."

"In the washtub?" asked Bessie, looking her up and down as if she didn't believe it.

"Washtub takes too much water," said Judy. "I can get clean in a molasses bucket, one arm and one leg at a time." She hoped Bessie wouldn't notice that her dress was unironed.

Bessie grunted and walked on. Other children from the shanties came along behind them. When they reached the school yard, they all went in together. A group of children already there sang out a greeting: "Here come the shanty kids! Here come the bean-pickers!"

Bessie took charge. To Judy and the children behind her, she said: "Don't none of you say a word." To the accusers, she replied calmly: "We don't pick beans and you know it."

"If you don't pick beans, you live on the drainage canal then."

"What of it?" answered Bessie. "What's the matter with that?"

"You live in shanties!" "You drink dirty water!" "You're hillbillies." "You wash your clothes in dirty water!" "You never been inside a house!" The teasing retorts came thick and fast.

Bessie marched over to the group and shook her fist in their faces. "Now, you Crackers, you can shut up for today. Hear me?" She turned to Judy. "Every day I got to shut these kids up. Just 'cause they live in real houses, they think they're better'n we are. We'll show 'em!"

The children stopped calling names and began to play games, with Bessie their leader. Bessie had more ideas and more initiative than all the others put together.

Judy stood off on one side and watched. Then she slipped over to the gate. She didn't like this school, after all. She decided to go home. Suddenly she turned and ran. Hearing footsteps behind her, she ran harder than ever. Then she felt a jerk on her arm and there was Bessie.

"Where you think you're goin'?" panted Bessie.

"Home," said Judy, frowning. "Don't like your ole school."

"Yes, you do," replied Bessie. "Them kids don't mean a thing. You gotta get used to 'em. You gotta talk back to 'em, to shut 'em up."

"What did you call 'em?" asked Judy.

"Crackers—they're mostly Crackers, born in Georgia or Florida. There's other kids from all over everywhere, too. They all shut up when I call 'em Crackers. You come on back with me."

Judy's heart sank. For the first time she was homesick for Alabama and the cotton fields and the little country school on Plumtree Creek. But Bessie marched her back to the schoolground. When the bell rang, Judy stayed close behind Bessie. Bessie took her in her own room, the Fifth Grade, and put her down beside her in her own seat. There were no empty seats.

The teacher, Miss Garvin, gave her one look and said: "Another new girl. From a crop family, I suppose. She won't know a thing."

She asked Judy her name and where she came from. Judy told her.

"If this class gets any larger," said Miss Garvin, "I don't know where we'll put the children. Where do you live?"

"On the . . . drainage . . . right next to Bessie Harmon," said Judy.

"Dirty bean-picker! Lives in a dirty ditch," whispered a boy behind her, loud enough for everybody to hear.

His taunts made Judy angry, and her shyness left her. She jumped up and faced the boy. "If you had to carry all your water, you'd be dirty yourself," she cried. "Plenty people in the United States don't have bathtubs with a million gallons of hot water to wash in." The words of the fortune-teller at the Alabama carnival came back to her. "Circus and carnival people don't have bathtubs. They travel around like folks who

[71]

harvest the crops. They wash in buckets and keep clean, and so do we."

The boy in the seat behind her was scared now. He hid his face in a book. Judy sat down. She was trembling all over.

"That's tellin' 'em!" whispered Bessie.

"Hot temper—no self-control," said Miss Garvin in a low voice. "Chip on her shoulder like all the rest."

Bessie handed Judy a Fifth Reader. "Study it," she said.

A shadow fell on the book and Miss Garvin was pointing to a sentence at the top of the page. "Well, let's see if you can read," she said.

Judy rose unsteadily to her feet. The words on the page

danced up and down. She could hardly see them. It had been so long since she had looked at words in a book. Bessie jerked her dress and said, "Read it out loud."

The words refused to stand still. Judy's hands shook so she nearly dropped the book. Miss Garvin lost patience and turned back to the first page. "Read *that*," she said, pointing.

When no response came from Judy's lips, Miss Garvin stared at her coldly. "How old did you say you are?"

"Ten," whispered Judy.

"Just as I thought. About ready for Third Grade," said Miss Garvin.

"But I finished the Third Reader at home and read part of the Fourth," Judy burst out.

"Down the hall, last door on your left, Third Grade, Miss Norris, teacher." Miss Garvin opened the door, a smile of relief on her face.

"But I wanted to stay with Bessie," gulped Judy.

"Bessie's in Fifth Grade, you're in Third."

Judy stepped out and the classroom door closed behind her.

But she did not go to Miss Norris's room. Instead, she tiptoed out of the building and ran home as fast as she could go. *I'll never go back to that school again! Never! I'll never go back!* The words echoed and re-echoed through her mind.

CHAPTER VI

The Canal Bank

Y OU must make a pen for that goat and shut her up nights or she'll git pneumonia and die, sure as my name's Patrick Joseph Timothy Mulligan."

"What can I make it out of?" asked Joe Bob.

"Go down to the dump and git some pieces of galvanized tin," said Mister Mulligan, "and drag 'em back here. Mighty fine place—that dump. No tellin' what you'll be a-findin' there."

"Will you go with me, Mister Mulligan?" asked Joe Bob.

"Not today, sonny," said the man. "My r-rheumatiz is better, thank the Lord, but I got such a rushin' of blood to me head, I might fall over any time day or night. Besides, I want to catch me a few catfish for a wee bite o' supper."

Joe Bob and Mister Mulligan had become great friends because they both liked to go fishing and to keep on fishing all day, whether they caught anything or not. Mister Mulligan had traveled all over the country, on foot, and now his feet were tired and had come to rest at last—in Florida.

Judy offered to go with Joe Bob. The dump was a long way off, and when they got there, it was enormous. It looked as if it held all the old worn-out cars and trucks in the world, also old stoves, machinery and refuse of all kinds. It was called: IKE'S JUNK YARD; and Ike, a tousled, rough-looking man, was kept busy watching to see that no visitor walked off without paying for what he took. People were wandering all over the dump. Men and boys were searching old cars for "parts." Small boys were hunting for wheels, axles, or unexpected treasures. A woman and a boy and girl were pulling an auto seat cushion behind them.

"Law me, I'm near about give out," said the woman, stopping to rest. "But this will be a heap sight better'n sleepin' on the hard, cold ground."

Judy recognized her. It was Mrs. Holloway who lived next door in a packing-box house. She was tall and thin and young, but had hardly any teeth.

"Howdy. How be ye?" she called cheerfully. "You-uns lookin' for a soft bed too?"

"No *ma'm*." Judy shook her head. "We got an iron bed in our tent. We're gittin' tin to make a shed for our goat."

"What do you-uns tote that noisy ole nanny goat around fur?"

asked Mrs. Holloway. "Smelly ole thing, do she eat up your tin cans?"

"No *ma'm*," said Judy. "She eats good green stuff and goat-chop, and she gives good milk for Lonnie to drink. Lonnie's not puny no more since he's been drinkin' goat's milk." She looked at the red-headed Holloway girl. "What's her name?"

"Tessie," answered the woman. "Tessie Henrietta Beulah Holloway."

"What's his'n?" Judy pointed to the little boy.

"Gwyn Lyle Holloway, same as his Pappy and Grandpappy and Great-grandpappy afore him."

"Funny names," said Judy.

"You-all talk funny too," said Joe Bob.

"I don't guess we can help how we talk," said Mrs. Holloway. "Hit depends on where you come from, don't it? Peo-

ple talk different in different parts of the country—you ought to hear how funny them Yankees talk *up north!*—but long as we can understand each other, we needn't pay no mind."

"Do people all talk different?" asked Judy. This was a new idea to her. "We're from Alabama. Where you-all from?"

"Windy Ridge up in the mountains of Tennessee," said the woman.

Judy left the Holloways and wandered off over the dump. She found a bent aluminum sauce-pan without a hole in it, then she saw a book and picked it up. Some of the pages were torn and soiled from rain, but it had pictures in it. She tucked it under her arm. She joined Joe Bob who had found several pieces of rusty corrugated tin. He was limping and Judy noticed he had blood below one knee.

"Did you hurt yourself?" she asked.

"Slipped and fell on some broken bottles," said Joe Bob. "Cut my leg but it don't hurt."

Ike asked the children to pay, but when they couldn't produce any money, he said crossly, "Take it then."

They dragged the tin home and Mister Mulligan admired it very much. From the junk piled up behind his little bird-box house, he produced some loose boards. He and Joe Bob set to work to make the goat shed.

Judy filled the battered sauce-pan with water and gave it to Missy to drink. Then she sat down to look at the book she had found. It was an old-fashioned Geography. On the front cover, beneath a picture of Christopher Columbus' three ships, she read the words: A NEW WORLD LIES BEFORE US. Judy studied these words and thought about what they meant. *When you are on the go all the time, how true it is—a new world always before you.*

She opened the book. It had colored maps and small engravings in black and white. One picture showed a steamboat loaded with bales of cotton and another, a field of sugar cane. Then there was a picture of two little colored boys, chewing cane stalks, just like Porky and Arlie back in Alabama. At the top of the page it said: The Southern States. *Why, it's all about our country!* said Judy to herself.

"Hey, sugarpie, what's that you got?" Papa came out of the tent carrying the foot piece of the iron bed.

"A book," said Judy. "I found it on the dump."

Papa laughed. "Want to go to town with me?"

"Can I have a quarter to buy feed for Missy?" asked Judy.

"Honey, look." Papa turned his pockets inside out, so she could see they were empty.

Papa had found some field work with a small grower several miles from town. But the money he made had to be used for food for the family, and the work hadn't lasted long.

"But I'll get you some money," Papa said. "You come along to town."

Papa put the head and foot pieces of the bed inside the jalopy and went back for the springs. Mama helped him lift them up on top of the car.

"Goodness gracious!" exclaimed Mrs. Harmon, coming

out to watch. "You folks pullin' out without tellin' me?"

"No ma'm," said Mama, then she paused.

"Well, you're not down to rock bottom yet," said Mrs. Harmon. "Nobody else on the canal has got a sewin'-machine *and* a Brussels carpet."

"My Grandma Wyatt lived in a *house*," bragged Judy.

"With Brussels carpet on the floor," added Papa. "Calla's folks had things nice. Why, that carpet cost a dollar thirty-nine a yard."

"No Jim," Mama corrected him. "It was a dollar sixty-nine, and Pa bought sixteen yards of it. That little piece is all I got left. I'll never part with it, nor with my sewin'-machine."

"Don't blame you none," said Mrs. Harmon. "I feel the same way about my rockin'-chair."

Mama looked at the bed on the jalopy and sighed. "I never thought I'd part with our iron bed——"

"*What you goin' to do with our bed, Papa?*" cried Judy. Suddenly she realized what was happening.

"Oh, you'll be glad it's gone," said Mrs. Harmon practically. "Nobody carries beds along. I bet there ain't another real bed along this whole canal. You folks is too high-toned! When you travel far like we do, you can't take beds and heavy stuff. You're lucky if you got a mattress. Plenty people depends on goin' to the town dump and huntin' up old seat cushions out of junked cars. They use 'em for beds and throw 'em back on the dump when they leave."

"Miz Holloway went to Ike's dump and got them an auto

seat to sleep on," said Judy in a low voice. She put her arm
around Mama's waist. "We still got a mattress."

"Come, Judy. Goin' with me?" called Papa.

The engine began to roar. Judy put her book inside the tent
and jumped in the jalopy. They drove straight to a second-
hand store. The man came out and helped Papa unload the
iron bed and take down the springs.

"Coulda give you a better price if you'd a brought the mattress, too," said the man.

"Gotta have somethin' to make the ground a little softer,"
laughed Papa. He came out of the store with his hand in his
pocket and a twinkle in his eye. He pulled out a quarter and
threw it in Judy's lap. "Down there's a feed store," he said,
pointing.

It was not One-Eyed Charlie's feed store, but it looked very
much like it. It smelled just the same, and feed sacks made of
printed cotton cloth were piled up inside. Judy bought her
grain and started out with it.

"That sack's pretty enough for a dress," she heard a man's
voice say behind her, "and there's a little girl who'd like to
have it."

Judy turned. A big burly farmer was having the contents
of several flowered sacks dumped into a larger one of burlap.
He kicked a sack in the girl's direction. "Take it," he called
out.

Quickly Judy rolled the sack up and tucked it under her arm.
"Thanks," she called back, hurrying out.

"What you been stealin', sugarpie?" asked Papa. "Somebody after you"

"Looky! Looky, Papa! Look what he gave me!"

The sack was dirty and saturated with dusty grain, but the printed pattern of pink and blue morning-glories could be plainly seen.

"I'll sew it on Mama's sewin'-machine," said Judy happily.

"My! Such a stylish lady you'll be," laughed Papa. Then he added, "Let's go get us each a coke."

They stopped in front of a drug store that had its whole front open on the street. They sat down at a table and drank their cokes in style. Across the street was a trailer camp. Hot-dog stands, lunch counters in tents and other concessions lined the sidewalk. Australian pine trees were planted along the

"streets" between the rows of trailers, which sat closely together.

The trailer camp looked beautiful, a great improvement on
the canal bank. Judy could see curtains at the windows and
clothes hung on tiny clothes-lines to dry.

"A house-trailer would be a good way to travel, Papa," she
said, "if you have to be on the go all the time. You'd have
a house of your own and you could take it right with
you."

"Yes, honey," said Papa. He sighed heavily. "They cost a
pile o' money, hundreds o' dollars."

They got up to go and Judy was sorry she had said what
she did. Papa was doing the best he could and there'd be a
job soon.

They walked along the street and looked in the show windows. It was a busy time and the sidewalk was crowded with
people. Suddenly, bearing down upon them, came a large fat
woman, hatless, with braids drooping over one shoulder. A
gathered skirt, with yards and yards of cloth in it, tumbled
about her. It was bright red, and her blouse was blue, with
stars and moons of silver on it.

Judy remembered like a flash. It was Madame Rosie, the
fortune-teller she had seen at the carnival in Alabama. Judy
took one look, then let go Papa's hand, turned and fled through
the crowd.

"Hey! Where you goin', honey?" Papa called after her.

But she was gone. And Papa was left facing a strange woman

he had never seen before. Madame Rosie took his arm and shook it vigorously.

"I been lookin' for you a long time, mister," she exclaimed. "Why don't you give that kid o' yours some decent food to eat—juicy steak and green vegetables and plenty milk to drink? Bet she hasn't had a drop o' milk today, now has she?"

Jim Drummond was puzzled. "No, Lonnie gits the milk," he said. "But what business is it of your'n? Who are YOU? She's *my* kid, not your'n."

"Look here, mister." Madame Rosie planted herself in front of the man and looked him straight in the eye. "You got a whole houseful o' kids, I bet, and you shouldn't have any at all, 'cause you're so ignorant you don't know how to feed 'em or bring 'em up properly."

"Now that's a nice thing to say to a man," began Papa weakly

But he didn't have a chance, for Madame Rosie continued: "You're that tall dark man I saw in that scared rabbit's life, and you'd better work harder and make things better for them kids, and give 'em a chance to go to school and read out of books with pictures in 'em." She stopped abruptly. "Where do you live? What you doin' here, so far from Alabama? 'Twas in Alabama I saw that girl before, I'll swear to it. Where's your home?"

"Ain't got none . . . yet," said Jim Drummond, dropping his eyes, "exceptin' the jalopy and tent."

"Livin' in a tent and haulin' them kids all over the country, no money and not even a steady job, I bet!" said Madame

Rosie. She shook her finger under his nose. "You just better settle down and get a home for that little scared rabbit . . . *with a picket fence round the garden like I saw.* . . . You better make that rabbit's fortune come true or I'll——"

Jim Drummond backed away, angry. "You're cuckoo! You're crazy! A fence? What you talkin' about a fence for? What I do is none of your business. You mind your own affairs or I'll have you arrested!"

Madame Rosie turned and went off across the street. Her shoulders heaved as if she were crying.

Jim Drummond shook his head. *She's crazy,* he thought to himself. But Madame Rosie's words stayed in his mind. He could not forget them. When he got back to the car, Judy was sitting hunched up in the seat, her lips set.

"Honey, did you ever see that woman before?" Papa asked.

"Yes, at that carnival we went to in Alabama," said Judy.

"Did you tell her we was poor, honey?"

"I never said a word to her, Papa," said Judy. "I was too scared to talk. I saw her sittin' in her tent. She tells fortunes for fifty cents."

Still Papa could not understand it.

"There! That's her tent there." Judy pointed across the street and read the sign: MADAME ROSIE—PALM READINGS —SPEAKS SEVEN LANGUAGES. She's part of that trailer camp, I reckon."

Papa was thoughtful. "Likely she can read our minds," he said.

Papa bought groceries on the way home, and when they got back, Judy displayed the feed sack. Mama put it in a bucket of water to soak the grain and dust out.

"Better not go near Missy with that feed-sack dress on," warned Papa. "She can smell that grain a mile off—even after you wash it out."

After supper the Holloways came over for a visit.

"We-uns come here winters and go up north summers," said Mr. Holloway. He was a tall, thin-cheeked mountain man. 'This-here's our fourth year."

"Up north? You mean back to Tennessee where you come from?" asked Papa.

"No," said Holloway. "I can't make me a living there. We go to South Jersey—big crop of peaches and vegetables there.

We-uns can git work steady the whole endurin' summer, but I don't see no sense to workin' when I don't feel like it. When a nice day comes along, I'm one to stop and enjoy it. We-uns cleared over five hundred dollars last season at that—me and the ole lady both pickin'. Bought us our car, a good un too."

"How'd you find out about goin' up there?" asked Papa.

"One feller, old neighbor o' mine from Newport, Tennessee, went first just to see what that-ere part of the world was like. He made a heap o' money and come on back home and told his neighbors. The next year other families went and tried it. Now there's a passel o' Tennessee folks go up thar every summer. They all come back with their pockets full o' cash for the winter."

"We-uns don't favor Tennessee in winter," said Mrs. Holloway. "Florida's more to our taste."

"That-ere farmer up in Jersey treats us fine for the most part," Holloway went on. "Gives us a two-story house to live in. . . ."

"A real house?" gasped Mama.

"Yes *ma'm*," said Mrs. Holloway.

"Better try Jersey come summer," said Holloway.

*   *   *

The next day Joe Bob and Mister Mulligan finished Missy's shed. They all went out to look at it. It had a wooden framework and tin on the top and two sides. Joe Bob was very proud of it.

"What you limping for?" asked Mrs. Harmon. "Hurt your-self?"

"Oh, it's nothin'," said the boy. He sat down and looked at his leg. "Jest a little bump and a cut."

The leg was badly swollen and the cut looked sore. When Joe Bob tried to get up, he could hardly walk.

"If I was you folks," said Mrs. Harmon, "I'd do something."

"What?" asked Mama, frightened. "What can we do?"

"They got a clinic over at the government camp in Belle Glade, and outsiders can go there for medical help," said Mrs. Harmon, "but that's a long ways from here. All you need is First Aid."

"What's that?" asked Mama.

"Good land! Don't you know?" asked Mrs. Harmon. "First Aid is gettin' that cut washed out good and clean, and bandaged so no germs can get in it."

"What's 'germs'?" asked Mama.

"I'll wash it," said Judy. "I'm not afraid of blood."

"I'd do it myself," said Mrs. Harmon, "but I'm afraid to use this canal water. It might infect it. There's only one thing to do—take him to school, to the school nurse. She'll fix it up. Better hurry and get there before school lets out."

"School?" gasped Judy. "They got a nurse at school? What'll she do to Joe Bob?"

"Good gracious, child, she won't hurt him none," said Mrs. Harmon. "Don't look so scared. She'll fix your brother's leg so it will get well quick. It don't pay to let a thing like that go. That cut's a deep one—she might have to take some stitches in it."

"You mean she'll sew it up?" demanded Judy, wide-eyed.

Joe Bob and Cora Jane began to cry. Then Lonnie started in.

"Calla, you stay here and get them kids quieted down," said Papa. "I'll take the boy to school, like Miz Harmon says. Judy can come too, and find the nurse."

"Just ask Bessie," said Mrs. Harmon. "She'll tell you where the nurse is."

Judy gulped. She would have to go back to school again.

It did not take long to get there in the jalopy, and school was not out yet. Judy went bravely in and Papa followed, carrying Joe Bob. He set him down by the door and they waited.

It was the hardest thing Judy ever did in her life—knock on the door of Miss Garvin's room. But knock she did.

"What? You back?" asked Miss Garvin. "Didn't I send you to Third Grade?"

"Bessie . . . I want Bessie . . ." stammered Judy. "My brother's hurt . . ."

Miss Garvin called Bessie, and almost before they knew it, they were all in the nurse's office. The nurse was little and pretty and her name was Miss Burnette. She examined Joe Bob's leg and said, "We'll fix that in a jiffy." She laid out adhesive tape and rolls of bandage. "But first we must wash it clean and disinfect it."

Joe Bob did not cry at all. He just watched what the nurse did.

[88]

"We was scared to wash it in canal water," said Judy.

"That was right," said Miss Burnette. "If you ever have to use water you are not sure of, boil it first." As she worked, she talked about the importance of cleanliness and of taking care of even minor injuries.

A man wearing a white coat came into the room.

"This boy has hurt his leg, Doctor," said the nurse.

The doctor set to work and before Joe Bob knew what had happened, it was all over. "Good thing to have a few stitches in that cut," said the doctor.

"Did . . . did you . . . sew me up, Doc?" asked Joe Bob, surprised.

"Yes," said the doctor, laughing.

"Come back in two days for another dressing," said Miss Burnette.

Joe Bob limped to the car with Papa's help. Then school was dismissed and Bessie climbed in the back seat with Judy.

Judy squeezed Bessie's arm. "Oh, I *do* like school after all!" she said.

CHAPTER VII

Bean Town

"JOE BOB'S leg is well again," announced Judy one day several weeks later. "The nurse took the bandage off."

Judy and Joe Bob stopped in at Mrs. Harmon's to pick up Lonnie. Lonnie was walking now and he stayed with Mrs. Harmon while Papa and Mama went to the bean house to work and the children were in school. Judy had bravely entered the Third Grade and was happy with her new teacher, Miss Norris.

"Land sakes!" said Mrs. Harmon. "So she did, and his leg looks as good as new."

All the canal children came running up and everybody looked at Joe Bob's leg.

"I'm going to be a nurse when I grow up," said Judy. "Just see what Miss Burnette gave me."

The children crowded close—Joe Bob, Cora Jane and Lonnie, Gwyn Holloway and Tessie with their baby sister in her arms, and the new twins, Roberta and Rosella Parish who had recently come to live on the canal bank. Judy displayed a First Aid kit.

"It's got everything in it—mercurochrome, adhesive tape and gauze for bandages," said Judy proudly. "Traveling around so much, Miss Burnette said we might need it. And she told me what to do with everything."

"My baby's got a cut on her finger," said Tessie Holloway.

"I'll fix it," said Judy. She washed the cut and bandaged it neatly.

"I got a baby too," said Rosella Parish. "I think she's got a cut, I'll go get her."

Soon seven-year-old Rosella came staggering out with a fat baby in her arms. "She ain't got a cut, but her hands are stuck shut, and she cries if you try to open 'em. Her toes are stuck together too, and her feet are sore."

"I can't fix that," said Judy, closing her kit. "You take her to the nurse at school. That's muck-sores. It comes from lettin' her play in the dirt—this black muck. It makes people's skin raw and sore. White people can't stand it to pick beans in the muck fields, their skin gets too sore. Even the colored people get it, but not so bad. Miss Burnette was tellin' about it. You take the baby to the clinic at school."

"I got a dozen mosquito bites," said Gwyn Holloway, but Judy had closed her kit.

"Read us outa your book, Judy," begged Tessie.

"Yes, let's play school," begged the others.

Judy put her First Aid kit inside the tent and brought out her Geography. She sat down on a crate and the children clustered round. They squirmed uneasily, scratching mosquito bites.

"Now children," began Judy, "what does it say on the book?"

"*'A New World Lies Before Us!'*" chanted the children in unison.

"And we want to learn all about the country we live in," added Judy. "Here's the map of the United States. Today I want each of you to tell me where you came from and we'll find it on the map."

First Joe Bob pointed out Troy, Alabama, then Tessie found Newport, Tennessee. The twins looked in Arkansas for Bald Knob but could not find it.

Just then Papa and Mama came home.

"Papa, we can't find it," said Judy. "Bald Knob just ain't in Arkansas at all."

The twins began to cry. "Yes it is! Yes it is! We came from there."

Papa took the Geography and looked all over the state of Arkansas. "It's there all right," he said. "I think it's that tiny little black speck. They just forgot to print the name."

The children all looked at the black speck and the twins were very proud. Then they looked for Lake Okeechobee and

[94]

Judy pointed out Bean Town. The children all put a finger on it. "That's where we are right now," they said.

"All of us here live in the Southern States," Judy went on. "When we study the New England States I'll show you where a girl in my class lives. Now tell me, what are the products of the Southern States?"

The children looked at each other. Nobody knew.

"What do they grow in the Southern States?" repeated Judy.

"Cotton," answered Joe Bob. "We used to pick it."

"Cotton," echoed the twins. "We picked it too."

"Sugar cane," said Gwyn Holloway.

"Cane syrup and 'lasses," added Tessie.

"Lumber—pine trees and turpentine," said Joe Bob. "We saw them tapping the trees in Georgia and North Florida. We saw turpentine camps."

After Judy read a few paragraphs aloud, the children began to shout all at once: "Oranges from Florida!" "Apples from Arkansas!" "Tobacco from North Carolina and Tennessee!" "Peaches from Georgia!" "Rice and salt from Louisiana!" "Cattle and wool from Texas!"

"Tomorrow we will study the rivers of the Southern States," said Judy. "Class dismissed." The children scattered and began to play.

"They're learnin' more outa that ole book than they do at school," said Mama.

"Judy has a way with her," said Mrs. Harmon. "Tells me she's gonna be a nurse when she grows up."

Mama laughed. "All because of Joe Bob's leg. Don't know which she likes the best, that school nurse or Miss Norris, her teacher. She's a big girl to be only in Third Grade, but she says there's some eleven and twelve years old in the class. They're from families who follow the crops and they miss a lot of school."

"She'll soon catch up to Fifth Grade where she belongs," said Mrs. Harmon, "if you folks stay here and keep her in school."

"That's just the trouble," sighed Mama. "We was countin' on steady work and gittin' a little cash money ahead. But it don't seem to be much. Each day the field hands can't start pickin' the beans till the vines dry off about eleven in the morning. We go to the bean house at noon and hang around, waitin' for the belts to start. Today they didn't start till two and then ran for only an hour. We git twenty-five cents an hour, so we made fifty cents—the two of us."

"What does Jim do in the bean house?" asked Mrs. Harmon.

"First one thing, then another," said Mama. "Sometimes he packs beans, sometimes he catches 'em, sometimes he works on a loading crew—that is, on the busy days. On slack days, the men just hang around like the women-folks."

"Yesterday you didn't work at all, did you?" asked Mrs. Harmon.

"No, on account of the rain they couldn't pick, so we didn't earn a penny. And every day the whole family's got to eat," said Mama. "If we can't earn more'n this, we'll have to move on, and that'll put the young uns back in their school work. Their Papa's set on 'em learnin' somethin'."

"Don't go yet," said Mrs. Harmon. "The peak of the bean season will soon be here, and then you can earn a-plenty and git caught up."

Mrs. Harmon was right.

Suddenly the crop reached its peak and the bean houses ran day and night, weekdays and Sundays. It was a rushing life. Papa and Mama were gone from noon till midnight, sometimes till 2 A.M. Then they would come in exhausted and throw themselves on the mattress without taking trouble to undress. Several times they did not get back until 5:30 the next morning. Judy took care of the children after school, got them their evening meal and put them to bed on their bundle of quilts. She was glad Mrs. Harmon was so near, at night.

The Drummonds needed money badly. Every extra hour that Mama and Papa could stick it out meant a few cents more. There was the back rent for camping on the canal bank and the always over-due grocery bill to be paid. New clothes were needed, and they must try to save a little. Nobody knew how long the peak of the bean harvest would last or what job would come next. The future was dark and uncertain.

Judy got used to having her parents away in the afternoon. Sometimes, coming back from school, she took Joe Bob and Cora Jane and walked through the main street of Bean Town to look in the show windows. They made up a game, picking out things in the windows that they liked best.

One day they met Madame Rosie. They came upon her so suddenly there was no escape. Madame Rosie bought them all double ice-cream cones and led them to her tent. Joe Bob and Cora Jane sat still, pretty scared, licking hard on their cones to keep them from dripping. Judy was surprised to find her shyness gone. It was as easy to talk to Madame Rosie as to Mrs. Harmon.

"You told my fortune once, didn't you?" said Judy.

"You bet, and a beautiful fortune I saw for you too, dearie," said Madame Rosie. "But tell me—what do you eat for breakfast?"

"Mama's workin' all night in the bean house now," said Judy. "She gets doggone tard watchin' them beans go by in the glarin' light and with all the noise of the machinery. She's so sleepy in the morning, sometimes she don't git up at all. I can cook fried bread as good as she can——"

" 'Fried bread,' what's that?" asked Madame Rosie sharply.

"It's jest self-risin' flour and water," said Judy. "You mix it with your hand and throw it in a skillet with grease."

"I never heard o' fried bread where I come from," said Madame Rosie.

"Where's that?" asked Judy eagerly.

"Well, from most everywhere," said the woman.

"Mister Mulligan comes from everywhere too," said Judy, "but he was born in Killarney, Ireland. I showed it to him on the map."

"Oh, I was born in Chicago, but——" began Madame Rosie.

"That's in the Central States," said Judy. "I'll bring my Geography and show you some time."

But Madame Rosie was more interested in food than in Geography, perhaps because she herself was so well fed. "What does that fried bread look like?" she persisted.

"It's a thick pancake, hard and solid. It bites hard, but it stays by you a long time," said Judy.

"Taste good?"

"Not very. It just fills you up."

"I thought you folks ate cornbread all the time. . . ."

"Mama says it's easier to buy a poke o' white flour, and Papa likes his biscuit and gravy, only Mama hasn't any oven to bake biscuit now."

"What did you eat for breakfast back home in Alabama?" asked Madame Rosie.

"Fried fatback and molasses and biscuit and gravy," said Judy. "That was before Papa swapped the oven."

"Good heavens! Never no milk nor orange juice?" cried Madame Rosie. "Think of bringin' up kids like that. It's a wonder they don't die. Must be tough stock."

"We got a goat," said Judy, "only she don't give much milk when we don't feed her grain. Just weeds and bushes don't make much milk, but what we git, Lonnie drinks it. And we had oranges once! That was when we lived by our little lake . . . I called it the Mirror of the Sky. . . ."

"Florida full of oranges . . . oranges rottin' on the ground in all the groves . . . and kids right here never gittin' a drop of orange juice!" mumbled Madame Rosie. "Can you beat that? Does your Mama ever cook any vegetables?"

"No *ma'm,* she don't have no time to cook," explained Judy. "At the bean house she can get all the 'culls' she wants—them's the beans that they throw out. Sometimes other things too—lettuce and cabbage and tomatoes and peppers—but she don't bother to bring them home no more. She ain't got no time to cook."

"Did you have a vegetable garden in Alabama?" asked Madame Rosie.

"*No ma'm,*" said Judy. "Old Man Reeves wouldn't let us. He made Papa plant cotton right up to the house on all sides. Said good cotton land shouldn't be wasted."

"What do you eat for supper while Mama's at the bean house?"

"Papa gives me a dime, or a quarter when he's got it, and we stop and buy hot-dogs and pop on our way home from school," said Judy.

"You can't cook?" asked Madame Rosie.

"No *ma'm,*" said Judy. "Miz Harmon asks us to supper sometimes. She lives next door, she's from Michigan—that's in the Central States. Bessie Harmon can cook—her Mama learned her how."

"You get Bessie to give you lessons," suggested Madame Rosie.

"But I ain't got no time either," said Judy. "I'm sewin'. Miz Harmon's helpin' me make my new dress. She's learnin' me to sew on Mama's sewin'-machine." Judy's face lighted up as she told about buying the goat with a dime, and how the goat brought her the feed sack for a new dress. "It'll be pretty, don't you think?"

"Yes I do," said Madame Rosie.

Then Judy told about Gloria Rathbone, the prettiest girl in the Third Grade, who was going to have a birthday party when she was nine years old, in a couple of weeks.

"I gotta go home and sew on my dress," said Judy. "I'm going to wear it to Gloria's party. Where do you think she's from? Connecticut! That's in the New England States."

Madame Rosie said goodbye and watched the little group disappear down the street. Joe Bob and Cora Jane hadn't said a word all through the visit, but they talked about the ice-cream cones all the way home. When they got there, Mama called from inside the tent. She was lying down and said she felt sick. Mrs. Harmon brought Lonnie in.

"I came back early," said Mama. "I told the boss that bean work was too rushing for a woman, and that I was sick and couldn't stand it no longer. He told me I needn't come back no more. I've lost my job, and the beans are beginning to play out. The belts only ran two hours today."

"Too bad," said Mrs. Harmon. "That's the way it goes. My folks was laid off last week. We're lucky we have so many of us can work. We earn enough to git by."

"We won't be movin' on, will we?" asked Judy anxiously.

"Gloria Rathbone's goin' to have a birthday party at her house and if I git my new dress done, I can wear it."

"When the boss laid me off, it made your Papa mad," said Mama. "He talked back to the boss and told him he wasn't treatin' us right and said he wouldn't work for him no more."

"*We ain't leavin', are we?*" cried Judy.

Suddenly the thought of moving on was more than she could bear. She remembered how awful the prospect of living on the canal bank had seemed when they first came. Now all that was changed. They had made a way of life in this dreadful and impossible place, and now that life seemed more desirable than any she had known before. There was the school, the nurse, the kind Third Grade teacher, Madame Rosie, the nice neighbors, the Geography book and the new dress. The canal bank had become *home*. *How could she leave all this and get used to being on the go again?*

"Papa's gone to git a job in celery," said Mama in a low voice.

"Hope he ain't rheumatic," said Mrs. Harmon. "He'll have to work in the wet all day in celery. Of course they furnish him rubber apron, boots and gloves. Work's heavier too than in beans and the shifts are sixteen hours at a stretch."

Mrs. Harmon went out. Mama turned her face to the tent wall.

"Oh, this ain't no way to live," said Mama in a dull voice. "Never no meetin' to go to, never no preachin' to listen to, never no all-day singin'. . . . A woman at the bean house told

me they have meetin' every Sunday at that government camp
at Belle Glade. Wisht we'd a gone there to live. They got runnin' water there too. . . ."

"We couldn't get in," said Judy. "That government camp
was plumb full. Don't you remember?"

"Oh, if only I could go to an all-day singin' once again. . . ."

Mama was homesick for Alabama and the little meeting-
house there. Judy could see that she was crying. She got out
her print cloth and tried to sew on the new dress, but she
couldn't enjoy it somehow.

The days passed. If Papa was over-tired from work in beans,
he became nervous and irritable after he started in celery. It
wasn't long until his joints began to ache, and he knew he
would have to get out of the wash house or come down with
rheumatism. His old longing to be outdoors came back in full
force.

"Here we are in the land of sunshine," he said to Mama one
day, "and we never see the sun. What good does it do us?"

"We're layin' by a little cash money," said Mama, trying to
be cheerful. "Remember that little farm we're goin' to git?"

"I'll be an ole man before I git it," said Papa bitterly. "I
feel like an ole man already I'm so sore in my joints."

* * *

Judy finished her new dress, and on Gloria Rathbone's ninth
birthday she wore it to school. It was made jumper style with
a gathered skirt, and a plain white blouse underneath. Mrs.
Harmon had given her the cloth for the blouse and Mrs.

Holloway had loaned her her iron to press them with.

Bright red cannas were blooming along the canal, and Judy gathered a bunch. When she gave them to Miss Norris, she noticed some girls pointing their fingers at her and whispering, but she was too happy to bother. All day she did good work, and Miss Norris told her that as soon as her Arithmetic caught up to her Reading, she could go in the Fourth Grade.

Judy beamed. She kept looking at Gloria—pretty Gloria with her soft blond curls clustered round her face. Gloria wore a silk dress today. The party was to be at Gloria's *house.* Judy wanted to see the house that Gloria lived in. She knew it would be a nice one and have carpet on the floor like Grandma Wyatt's. It was a long time since she had been in a house.

At last school was dismissed and all the children hurried out. Judy waited by the side door until Joe Bob and Cora Jane came, and got them started on their way home alone. Then she looked for Gloria and the other Third Graders.

They were going out the gate on the other side of the school yard. They had their arms linked around each other's waists and Gloria with the sunshine hair was in the middle.

"Glor-ia! Glor-ia!" called Judy. She called Beverly and Alice and Betty Anne by name too.

But they kept right on going.

"Wait for me, Gloria!" sang out Judy. "I'm coming to your birthday party too!"

Gloria and the other girls turned their heads and looked back. Then they started to run off down the street.

Judy stopped, overcome. They didn't want her. They were running away from her. She couldn't believe it. She refused to believe it. She chased the girls and caught up close behind them.

Then Gloria switched around and said haughtily, "What do *you* want? Why are *you* coming with us, I'd like to know?"

"I made . . . my new dress . . . to wear to your birthday p-p-par-ty, Gloria," stammered Judy. "I've never been to a party in all my life——"

"You're not invited!" Gloria stamped her foot on the sidewalk. She wore new patent-leather slippers today. "I don't want you—in your old feed-sack dress! And your dirty bare feet—I suppose you don't even own a pair of shoes. Who'd want a big, overgrown bean-picker at their party? *I* don't, so there!"

Beverly and Alice and Betty Anne and the others all linked

arms again with Gloria in the middle. They went skipping off down the street.

Judy stood there. She had to believe it now—Gloria had said it plainly enough. She wasn't invited. You had to be *invited*, to go to a birthday party. Judy didn't know that before. She looked down at her bare feet. They were stained and dirty. She had washed them clean the night before, but she had never once thought of shoes. Her new dress had taken all her attention. Of course you couldn't go to a party without shoes. That was it. You had to have shoes to be invited.

She walked slowly home. Bessie Harmon caught up with her and asked what was wrong. Judy told her everything.

"Aw—what do you bother with them little babies for?" said Bessie. "You'll go through the Fourth Grade in no time, and then you'll be in Fifth, with girls your own age. That little Gloria Rathbone's a snooty Yankee from Hartford, Connecticut. Thinks she's the whole cheese because her father owns one of these big packing plants down here."

A Yankee! Judy thought of the things her parents had said about mean, thieving Yankees. It couldn't be true—Gloria was so pretty and Judy had liked her so much . . .

"Bet she's a dumb-bell," Bessie went on. "Does she ever know her lessons?"

"She don't know her multiplication table yet," said Judy, "and I been helpin' her with her spelling."

"Aw—forget her then," said practical Bessie. "Hope you sassed her good."

"No, I never said a word," admitted Judy.

The thought comforted her. For once, when she might have said many things to be sorry for, she had held her tongue.

Judy felt better after listening to Bessie. But she wondered what she would tell all the children along the canal. They would all want to hear about the party and see what she had brought for them.

But when she got home, nobody asked her anything. Something more important was happening. The party faded away.

Papa! Mama! Are we leaving? She tried to find the words but couldn't.

She saw in one glance that the place where the tent had been standing was empty, and that the jalopy and trailer were loaded. Missy was in the trailer, bleating noisily.

All the neighbors were crowding round to say goodbye. Papa and Mama and the children were already in their seats. They were waiting for her to come.

"Goodbye, goodbye," called Bessie and her mother. "See you down here again next winter."

"Goodbye, goodbye," called the Holloways. "We'll meet you in New Jersey."

Goodbye! Good luck!" called Mister Mulligan.

Over the sound of the engine Judy could hear the neighbors' voices, but she could not see them. Her eyes were blurred with tears.

"We're on the go again," she whispered to herself.

CHAPTER VIII

Oleander

"PAPA," said Judy, "are we goin' to git us a farm?"

"With a cow and a mule and a dog and a cat?" asked Joe Bob.

"Not jest yet," said Papa, laughing. "We gotta make more money first."

"Where we goin' this time?" asked Cora Jane.

"Up north," answered Papa.

Papa was gay again, now that they had started going somewhere. He seemed more like himself than he had for a long time. It was April—real summer weather in Florida, but not yet too warm. Papa had decided to leave Bean Town before the end of the bean harvest, when all the other workers would be leaving.

"We'll be like the redbirds and bluebirds and robins," said
Papa. "We'll go up north for the summer. They say it gits so
all-fired hot down here nobody can stand it. And there's no
work, so the Negroes go north by big truckloads. They follow
potato and other vegetable crops along the Atlantic seaboard.
All the big Florida vegetable fields are flooded by summer
rains. The growers have to pump the water off and drain the
land, before they can begin planting again in September."

"Will we come back to Florida next winter?" asked Joe Bob.

"Depends on what we find up north," said Papa.

"Are we going up north?" cried Judy.

Up north was a far away and very mysterious place, but it
had somehow changed character. It was not so much the home
of Yankees who had burned your great-grandmother's house
and stolen her silver, but of strange people who consumed tons
of oranges, beans, celery and other vegetables.

"Will we git us a farm *up north,* Papa?" asked Judy.

"Law, no," said Papa, "but I hope I'll git some of that Yankee
money in my pocket."

"I never went to Gloria Rathbone's party, after all," said
Judy.

"Why not?" demanded Joe Bob. "You promised to bring
me somethin'."

Judy bristled. "That mean little ole Gloria called me names,"
she explained. "Said nobody couldn't come to her party who
wasn't invited. I never even saw the house she lives in. Didn't
want to see her wonderful ole house neither."

"I call that a low-down Yankee trick," growled Papa.

"She's a Yankee all right, Bessie Harmon said so," Judy went on. "Just because her father owns a bean house, she thinks she's smart. But I had to help her with her multiplication table and her spelling. She wore a silk dress and had new patent-leather shoes too."

"Bet your new dress was prettier than hers, honey," said Papa.

"Nobody looked at it," mourned Judy. After a pause she added, "I never did see Lake Okeechobee once. I never went up on the dike."

"And I never caught nothin' but catfish in that little ole dirty canal," said Joe Bob.

It was good to leave the flat, level sawgrass and elderberry land of the Glades and the unending miles of vegetable fields. It was good to get away from the great treeless stretches of muck and swamp. Soon there were shiny-leaved citrus groves again and towns with shady streets to rest the eyes from the sun. The towns were full of white houses and green grass lawns with sprinklers going, and bright-colored flowers blooming— azalea, hibiscus, flame-vine and bougainvillea.

"We'll take Holloway's advice and go to New Jersey," said Papa, consulting the map. "Route 17 is what we want—the shore route through Georgia and the Carolinas. If we see anything promising along the way, we can always stop. No use shootin' through like a railroad train. Mama don't feel so good so we'll jest mosey along."

The first night they camped on a side road, and Papa and Joe Bob caught a mess of fish in a pond near by. Blue herons waded in the water along the shore. The night was warm and the frogs kept up a continuous chant, *yank—y pank—yank— y—pank,* which soothed everybody to sleep.

The next morning they stopped in the nearest town. The streets were lined with large bushes, whose pink and white blossoms were beginning to open. Mama and Papa took Lonnie into a grocery store to buy food, while the children waited in the jalopy. Judy reached out and picked a sprig off the bush by the car, with a cluster of pink flowers on it.

"You like them posies?" asked a woman's voice.

"Yes *ma'm,*" said Judy shyly.

The woman, who wore a long skirt and a man's wide-brimmed straw hat, had come across the street. She stopped by the loaded car.

"You can root it easy," she said. "Jest keep the stem in a bottle o' water till the roots start growin', then set it out. Did you ever root any 'slips'?"

"No *ma'm,*" said Judy. "Never heard o' 'em before. Never saw no posies like these before."

"They're called *oleanders,*" said the woman. "We named our town for 'em—Oleander."

"I think it's the nicest town in the whole world," said Judy impulsively. "Wisht we could live here always. Wisht we could git us a farm here . . ."

"Where do you live?" asked the woman.

"Nowheres," broke in Joe Bob bitterly. "Different place every night."

"We're all the time on the go," said Judy.

"Where's your *home?*" asked the woman, looking at the car's license plate.

"It *was* in Alabama, but it ain't no more," said Judy. "We're lookin' for Papa a job."

"What kind of a job?" asked the woman.

"Outdoors," said Judy. "Papa don't like machinery nor factory work. He don't want to be whistled in and whistled out. All he knows to do is farm."

"Can he pick tomatoes and cucumbers?" asked the woman.

"Yes *ma'm!*" smiled Judy. "Best picker that ever was. I can pick too. So can Joe Bob, but Cora Jane's too little. We used to pick cotton."

"When your father comes, you tell him to come to my place and see my husband," said the woman. "We need help bad. Go out the main road four miles and look for a mailbox that says GIBSON on it. That's us. I got a girl, Mary John, just your age. Remember the name: GIBSON." She hurried away.

Judy and Joe Bob looked at each other, then they burst out laughing. "We got Papa a job!" they cried. They began to dance up and down. Joe Bob bumped against the horn and it began to honk.

Papa and Mama came running.

"What's the matter? What you done done? Anybody hurt?"

"No," said Judy. She whispered to Joe Bob. "Don't tell yet. Let's make 'em guess."

Papa and Mama put the groceries in the car. Papa's face looked sad.

"Looks like good farm country round here, but they must be small farms if they don't use outside help," he said. "That man I talked to said if he needs help, he jest calls on his neighbors. This is their peak season right now for about six weeks, for cucumbers and tomatoes. The other feller with him said there's a big harvest of potatoes up in the St. Johns River section, south of Jacksonville."

Mama got out the map. "Up here somewheres," she said, pointing with her finger.

"We'd ought to make that in a day, if we keep goin'," said Papa. He started the motor and the throbbing of the engine began to shake the car.

"Better tell 'im," whispered Joe Bob, "or he'll go on past."

"Papa!" screamed Judy, trying to make herself heard. "Stop at Gibson's four miles out. It says GIBSON on the mailbox. Watch for it—don't go too fast."

"What for?" asked Papa, when the engine had quieted a little.

"I got a job for you—outdoors too!" said Judy proudly.

"A JOB?" laughed Papa.

They were there in a few minutes. The mailbox said GIB-SON in large letters.

The first thing Judy looked at was the house. It was not one of the big white-pillared mansions she had seen in Alabama and Georgia. It was a weathered gray two-story farmhouse with a wide verandah running round three sides, set back from the road. The driveway was bordered with vine- and moss-draped oaks, and the yard was bright with flowering shrubs and bottle-bordered flower beds of phlox and petunias. Two huge clumps of oleander, coming into bloom, grew on each side.

"I think it's the nicest house in the world!" exclaimed Judy.

There was Mrs. Gibson, brush-broom in hand, sweeping the sandy yard between the flower beds. And there was her daughter, Mary John, chubby and round, with blue eyes and yellow hair.

"You made good time," said Mrs. Gibson.

"What's all this?" asked Papa, bewildered.

Mrs. Gibson explained that her husband had fallen from his tractor and broken his leg in two places, and was kept to his bed. He had three acres in tomatoes and two acres in cucumbers, both ready to be harvested, besides peppers and other vegetables coming along. She took Papa in the house to talk to Mr. Gibson, and when he came out again, he was all smiles.

"Where did you say we should put up our tent, ma'm?" he asked.

Mrs. Gibson pointed out a shady spot under a mossy live oak a short distance from the house.

"Hit's right near the well and the garden and the grove," she said. "That's a flowin' well there—best water in the world —never stops runnin'. You-all can have all the oranges and vegetables you want. Just help yourself."

Mama was so surprised she was speechless. She had never met any one like Mrs. Gibson before—so brisk, energetic, untiring and kind. Mrs. Gibson treated people well and expected to be well-treated in return. Since her husband's accident, she was managing the farm with the help of one man, Ollie Peters.

To Judy it was like a dream come true.

"Bessie Harmon told me folks born in Florida are called Crackers," she said to Mary John. "Are you a Cracker too?"

Mary John was shy. "I reckon I am," she drawled.

"My school in Bean Town had Crackers," said Judy, "and

other kinds too, from all over the country. One girl was from Connecticut."

Mary John smiled. "That was nice."

"How come you got a boy's name *John?*" asked Judy.

"I'm named for my Daddy," said the girl.

They were friends at once. Mary John gave Judy 'slips' from her mother's plants and empty tin cans to grow them in. Judy started a flower bed in front of the tent.

"Can I take them along with me when we go?" she asked.

"Oh, but you're going to stay here," insisted Mary John.

Mrs. Gibson asked the Drummond children to come in often for supper. They learned to sit down at a table and to eat with forks instead of their fingers or spoons. Sometimes Judy and Mary John watched Mrs. Gibson at her cooking or baking. Mrs. Gibson had a large, old-fashioned range and she would put two chicken pies and several pans of soda biscuits and crackling cornbread in the oven at once. She always had baked or boiled sweet potatoes on hand for the children to eat. Once Judy and Mary John mixed a cake and baked it. When it was done, the children had it to eat all to themselves. Judy had never known such a kitchen. It gave the word *home* a new meaning.

Papa began work right away and he had plenty to keep him busy. But he was happier than he had been for a long time because he could be outdoors and because he had some responsibility of his own.

The tomatoes and cucumbers had to be hauled in Mr. Gib

son's truck to the State Farmers Market in Oleander, where
they were auctioned off to the highest bidder. But first they
had to be picked. The cucumbers could not be picked in the
morning because the dew on them would cause them to rust.
So they were picked in the afternoon and the tomatoes were
picked, green, in the morning. Ollie Peters showed Papa everything. The two men took turns driving the truck to the market
each morning about eleven o'clock.

Both crops came on with such a rush that Mama and the
children went out in the tomato field to help pick. Judy missed
Mary John, who was going to school every day, but she was

anxious to help Papa keep his job. Lonnie and Cora Jane
played in the paths or sat in the shade at the end of the rows,
while Mama and Judy and Joe Bob picked.

At first it was fun to fill up the baskets. But Ollie Peters
shook his head when he saw the children tossing the green
tomatoes.

"Put each one down carefully," he said, "so you don't
bruise it. Them buyers at the market are mighty fussy."

The baskets were heavy to move. The vines that had not
been staked were lying sprawled on the ground, and that meant
stooping. The green sap from leaves and stem stained their
hands a dark green. The sun grew hotter as the days passed.
Judy was always glad to see the truck go out of the field at
eleven each morning.

One day toward the end of April she went along with Papa
riding high up in the front seat.

The market was a busy place. Under a vast open shed, hundreds of autos, trucks, horse- or mule-drawn vehicles gathered
and waited in line. Over at one corner was the "auction block,"
where the buyers began bidding, at twelve noon, on each lot
brought in. It took a long time for Papa's turn to come. Papa
bought sandwiches and pop to pass away the time.

"Do you have to wait like this every day?" asked Judy.

"Shore do," said Papa. "Suits me fine. I'll tell you a secret,
honey. If it wasn't for this chance to rest in the middle of the
day, I could never keep up with Mr. Gibson's crops."

"But it's outdoor work like you wanted . . ." began Judy.

"Shore," said Papa. "It's fine, and if I don't get tuckered out, we'll git cash money ahead and a little nest-egg to put in Mama's stockin', just 'cause my little gal got her Papa a job."

Judy beamed with happiness. "I'd like to go to school with Mary John, but I won't start till after the cukes and tomatoes are all sold," she said. "I'll keep right on pickin' no matter how tard I git."

"Now, sugar, you needn't over-do it," said Papa. "When I git ahead a little, I'll see that you go to school every day."

The line of cars began to move and Papa started the truck engine. Soon they came to the 'block.' A colored man lifted off a crate of cucumbers and another of tomatoes, and they were dumped out as samples. The auctioneer began 'crying the sale,' and the buyers walking about on the platform began their mysterious silent bidding—nodding, winking or whispering their bids. Judy could understand none of it, and in a moment it was all over. A slip of paper was handed to Papa and he drove to the other side of the building to unload and get the cash money paid for the load. He showed Judy a platform at the back where the green tomatoes were being graded, wrapped and packed for immediate shipment.

Then they were on the road again for home.

"Looks like we'd be gittin' rain," said Papa.

"Why, the sun was shinin' all the way in to town," said Judy.

A large black cloud had gathered overhead and the whole

sky was overcast. The wind began to blow. A drizzle started, which soon turned to heavy rain. The wind increased, accompanied by lightning and a dull rumble of thunder.

"The rain'll be good for the cukes," shouted Papa. "Ollie's been sayin' they'd git played out, if we didn't have rain soon."

Judy couldn't say anything, the wind was blowing so hard. She had never seen anything like it. Loose sticks and palm branches were blown high into the air. Trees were bent over to the ground and many of them snapped off. The rain came down in torrents, turning suddenly colder. She wished for her coat—her old winter coat that she had hardly worn twice since she came to Florida.

The rain poured in through the open truck window and drenched her. It plastered her hair down to her head. She moved over closer to Papa, but that didn't help much. Then

it began to hail. The road ahead became covered with bouncing white balls of ice. All other cars seemed to have disappeared. Theirs was the only car on the road.

"Hens' eggs!" shouted Papa, laughing.

But Judy couldn't hear what he said.

They reached home at last, but had to stop before they got halfway down the Gibsons' driveway. Papa shut off the engine and they looked. A large palm tree lay across their path. The tent under the live-oak was squashed flat by a huge branch from overhead.

Judy gasped. "Where's Mama?" she cried.

"In the house, of course," said Papa. He took Judy by the hand and ran with her to the Gibsons' verandah. The door opened to let them in and was closed swiftly behind them, to keep the wind out. Mama and the children were all safe inside. Mrs. Gibson brought dry clothes for Papa and Judy to change to.

The hail storm ended everything.

"Eight hailstones hit every tomato," said Ollie Peters, laughing, after the storm was over. But it was no laughing matter. The tomato plants were completely broken down and the cucumbers destroyed. Mr. Gibson's loss was over a thousand dollars.

"The first rain after a dry spell," said Ollie, "we're shore to git hail. Hit's because the sand is so dry. Funny storm too —a little streak only half a mile wide, but it smacked us right in the face."

The Gibsons' loss was so great, the Drummonds couldn't say a word about their own.

It took several days to dry the mattress out. The kerosene stove and the sewing-machine weren't hurt except for rust. The tent was torn in two, but Mrs. Gibson and Mama sewed it up again. All the clothes got a soaking, but the sun came out and dried them.

It was hard to say goodbye to the Gibsons or to know how to thank them. You couldn't thank people for treating you like human beings. They would always be in debt to the Gibsons, the kind of debt they could never repay—the debt of kindness.

Everybody was sorry the work had ended so soon. There was nothing to do but pack up and get started. Mary John brought over a big box of sandwiches and a sack of oranges for the trip. She brought half a dozen plants in small tin cans, to take the place of those destroyed in the hailstorm. She put a slip of oleander in Judy's blue bottle and tied it by a string just inside the car window.

With her arm around Mary John's waist, Judy had one last visit to the kitchen that smelled of all the good things that had been cooked in it. She came out and took one last look at the flowers on the verandah and in the yard, and one last look at the Gibsons' house. Then she threw her arms around Mary John and hugged her tight.

Honk! Honk! Joe Bob was honking the horn.

Judy ran to the car. Papa started the engine and the Drummonds were on the go again.

CHAPTER IX

Georgia

"OH PAPA, can't we tote it in the trailer?" begged Joe Bob.
"We'd git plenty milk if we had a goat *and* a cow,"
said Judy.

"One animal's enough," said Papa. "Besides, that heifer calf
don't belong to us. The owner'll come and git it himself. Right
here on the main road—everybody's seen it."

The Drummonds were looking at a new baby calf that was
sleeping in the corner of the rail fence. The jalopy engine was
hot and Papa was letting it cool off.

"Reckon I'll have to push her back to that gas station," said
Papa, "and see if I can git that fan belt fixed."

Papa unhitched the trailer and began to push the car along
the side of the road. Mama steered and Judy and Joe Bob

helped push. At last they got there. Two men were sitting on chairs tipped back against the building. Several pigs were wallowing in the dust and two cows were standing in the shade under the roof.

"Whew!" exclaimed Papa, wiping the sweat off his forehead. "Nice shady place you-all got here."

"Yep!" said one of the men, spitting into the dust.

"Been havin' dry weather, I see," said Papa.

"Shore have," said the man.

"Can I roll my jalopy in under the shade?" asked Papa.

"Pervided you don't run over the livestock," laughed the man.

"Been havin' trouble with my fan belt," said Papa.

Mama took the children inside and bought them some peanuts. There was no place to sit down inside, so she came out again. The children found sticks and started chasing the pigs.

"Ju-dy! Ju-dy!" called Mama suddenly, but her voice sounded strange and weak.

"Ju-dy!" called Papa sharply. "Take care o' Mama. My hands are covered with grease."

Judy thrust the peanut bag in Joe Bob's hands and ran to her mother's side. Mama looked pale. "Git me a chair, gal, before . . . I faint. . . ."

Judy looked swiftly. There were no chairs except those on which the two men were sitting.

"Hey, mister," cried Judy, "can't you see my mother's sick? *Git off that chair and let her sit down!*"

Startled, the man got up and backed sheepishly away. The second man got up too. Mama slipped down on the nearest chair. "Water . . . a drink . . ." she murmured. Judy ran to a pump at one side of the building and filled a tin cup she found there. Mama sipped it and opened her eyes again. Judy pulled the other chair over and sat close to Mama.

"Feelin' better, Calla?" called Papa.

"It's jest the heat," said Mama. "Soon's we git goin', I'll be all right."

Papa worked a long time on the car. Judy picked up a newspaper that one of the men had been reading and fanned Mama's hot face. After a while, she opened it and glanced idly through it.

"Oh Papa, here's an ad in big letters," said Judy. "'BEAN PICKERS WANTED, Charleston, S. C., April 15-May 15. Good wages.'"

Papa cocked his head and listened. Judy put the paper down.

Cars and trucks kept going past and often one would stop for gas. The tall man, who wore a black felt hat, set the gas pumps going and put air in tires when it was asked for. Suddenly a large truck rolled by and the echo of a song sung by a number of people floated through the air.

"What was that?" inquired Papa.

"People singin' in that truck," said the short man.

"Sounded like colored folks in the fields back home," said Mama. "Enough to make a body homesick."

"They're goin' up north to work in the crops," said the black-hatted man. "They're bean-pickers—been pickin' beans in Florida all winter. They go clear up to Jersey and New York State."

Another truck came by more slowly, to the sound of talking and laughing. The sides were high and the top was covered with a large canvas.

"They got women and children in there—whole families, squeezed in like sardines in a box," said the tall man. "Top's covered over to keep the rain off."

"In dry weather like this?" laughed Papa. "Looky there, it's stopping."

The second truck had stopped a short distance away.

"They most generally never stop," said the short man, scratching his head. "They go whizzin' right through—keep goin' day and night, never stop to eat or drink or nothin'. Wonder what's happened."

The Negroes were piling out of the truck, glad of a chance to stretch and walk about. The short man went down the road to see if the truck needed repair. Some of the people came to the gas station, to get drinks of water at the pump.

Judy saw a little girl who made her think of Pinky Jenkins. She had bright eyes and her hair was braided in many tiny braids.

"What's your name?" asked Judy.

"Rose Ann Davis," said the girl. "I's tired sittin' on that narrow plank. No place to lay your head or go to sleep. My little brother, Ed Willie, he sleeps on the floor under the plank."

"Where you goin'?" asked Judy.

"Dunno," said Rose Ann. "Up north to work in the crops."

"You're too little to work, ain't you?" said Judy.

"I's seven," said Rose Ann, "but I can pick five hampers o' beans in a day. My Mammy likes to have me help her. I's a good bean-picker."

The crew leader, in charge of the load, blew a whistle and the people hurried back to the truck. The garage man returned.

"That's worse than the way they used to haul cattle on the railroad trains," he said. "They're goin' through to New York State. I pity 'em time they git there."

Papa looked at Mama. "Feelin' better now, honey?" Mama nodded. "Ain't we the lucky ones to have a car of our own?"

They all climbed in the jalopy, rode to the trailer and after hooking it up, they started. On and on they went, passing pine woods, fields and settlements, and crossing frequent bridges.

"Wisht I could stop and ketch us a bait o' fish for supper," said Joe Bob.

"We've lost so much time already," said Papa, "we can't stop for nothin' now."

"Unless it's me," said Mama.

"We'll stop if you don't feel good, Calla," said Papa.

A huge snake was worming its way across the road ahead. Papa swerved just in time to avoid hitting it. Then he drove onto a long rickety wooden bridge over a wide stretch of cypress swamp. Soon the engine began to spout water and heat up.

"Gosh almighty!" said Papa. "There she goes again. Thought I had that fan belt fixed. Can't stop on this narrow bridge . . ."

The traffic moved slowly, a long line of cars and trucks ahead and more behind. Another long line was going slowly in the other direction. The jalopy kept going, spouting more and more steam.

"Jim," said Mama. "Let's find a place to stop soon. I gotta lie down."

"Yes Calla," said Papa. "Soon's we get outa this funeral procession."

After the bridge was crossed, the road was smoother and it was lined on both sides with pine forests, but there were no turns or side roads. Suddenly the jalopy stopped. Mama said she couldn't go any farther. That settled it.

A little ahead was a railroad crossing. The woods beside the road was a swamp, a foot deep in water. The only dry place was the grassy slope at the edge of the highway. Papa parked the jalopy and trailer on the slope. He staked the goat farther down. Judy cleared out the back seat of the car and Mama lay down and went to sleep. So did Lonnie and Cora Jane in front.

It was still mid-afternoon. Among the things removed from the car, Judy found the tin cans that held Mary John Gibson's slips. They were dry and wilted, and so, while she hated to do it, she threw them away. The oleander slip in the blue bottle had started to root. She looked in the grocery basket to see what there was to eat. She found a dry piece of bread, and she and Joe Bob took turns, biting.

Papa opened the hood of the car to let the engine cool off. "Judy gal," he called, "come here, listen. You and Joe Bob must go buy me a new fan belt." He gave her some money. "Go down to the railroad track and follow it till you come to the next town. I see smoke down there. That means there's a mill or turpentine still or somethin', so it must be a town. Go to the first garage you see and ask for a fan belt for a Ford. When you come back, watch for this paved road and the jalopy."

"I could stay with Mama," said Judy. "You could walk faster, Papa."

"No," said Papa. " 'Tain't safe for me to leave your Mama

sick and the young uns sleepin' so close to the highway. You and Joe Bob go do it."

"Come on, Judy," called Joe Bob.

They went to the railroad crossing and started off to the right, walking the railroad ties. Soon they were blotted out of their father's sight by the thicket of tall pine trees.

There was nothing Papa could do to the car, so he sat down on the running board to rest. He decided not to put the tent up until nearly dark. He noticed people in passing cars looking and pointing, but he paid no attention. After a while a big car pulled up. Two well-dressed men were sitting on the front seat. One of them inquired: "What do you call this?"

"Howdy!" said Papa. "I'm jest gittin' ready to camp here for the night. I'm drivin' up north, but been havin' trouble with my car and can't go no further."

"Can't park on the highway," growled the man. "You'll have to move on. You're blockin' traffic."

"But I'm *off* the highway," said Papa.

"Sorry, mister, but this is against the law." The man opened his coat to show the star on his vest. "I'm county sheriff. This man with me belongs to the State Police."

"But my wife's sick!" protested Papa. "She's in the car, sick, and my car's broke down. It won't go till I git a new fan belt."

"Sorry. Git goin' soon's you can." They drove on.

Mama was awakened by the sound of the men's voices and heard what they said. Sick as she was, she got up and packed the stuff back in the car, while Papa put the goat in the trailer.

[130]

"If them kids would only come," sighed Papa.

But they did not come.

A small truck slowed up and a pleasant voice called out, "In trouble, neighbor? Can I help?"

"Where's the nearest town?" asked Papa. "Garage there?"

"Swampville, two miles," said the man. "Best garage in the county. Can I tow you in? I've got a good chain handy."

"Thanks," said Papa. "This is luck."

The two men fastened the tow line and Papa climbed in the jalopy beside Mama and the little ones.

"Won't we wait for Joe Bob and Judy?" asked Mama.

"Can't," said Papa. "Likely we'll ketch up with 'em in town."

* * *

Meanwhile Judy and her brother had followed the railroad track till they came to Swampville. They had no difficulty locating the garage and getting the fan belt. While they were there, they heard a long freight train go through the town. They started back the way they had come. Sometimes they stepped on the railroad ties, counting them. Sometimes they tiptoed along on the shiny rails. They liked walking the railroad track.

"What are those big birds?" asked Joe Bob, looking ahead.

Large black birds were circling around above the tracks, now and then dipping low to the ground.

"Don't you know? Turkey buzzards!" exclaimed Judy with disgust. "They're after a dead cow or hog, I reckon. Likely

[131]

that train ran over it. These old range critters go anywhere they've a mind to."

By the time the children came up, the buzzards were hopping about awkwardly on the ground. They looked like big black turkeys, with bald heads. As the children approached, they flopped about before starting to fly away, frightened.

Joe Bob ran to the ditch below the track. It was not a cow or a hog.

"It's a dog, somebody's dog," he said in a low voice. "Oh, I wisht I'd a had that dog for my own . . ."

"Is he done dead?"

Judy wheeled around at the sound of a strange voice. There stood a small, ragged boy, wearing a torn straw hat. She had not seen him before and wondered how he had slipped up so quietly.

"Dog's been run over," she said. "Train musta threw him in the ditch. We seen them buzzards. Where'd you come from?"

The boy pointed toward the pine woods beside the tracks. The trees had had broad gashes chipped off on one side, and earthenware cups were attached to catch the slow-moving gum. No houses could be seen.

"Where do you live?" Judy asked again.

The boy did not answer.

Joe Bob stood looking at the dead dog. "Musta been a nice dog," he said. "Wisht we could bury him, so them buzzards won't eat him."

"There's a hole over yonder," said the ragged boy, "where

a tree's been uprooted. If we-uns could git him over there . . ."

The children found a fallen branch of a cabbage palm, shoved the dog onto its broad, strong leaf, and dragged it over into the woods. They put the dog in the hole, and dug dirt loose with their hands to cover it. It took a long time to fill the hole. Then they piled sticks and branches on top.

The ragged boy was silent the whole time. Then he started off through the woods.

"Where you goin'?" asked Judy.

"Back to work," said the boy.

"What work?"

"Cuppin' and dippin'," came the answer. "Pa does the chippin'."

"What's that?"

The boy took a gum-filled cup from the slashed side of a pine tree and poured it slowly into a wooden bucket that sat on the ground. The bucket was almost full. It was all he could do to carry it to the next tree.

"Hit's gittin' heavy," said the boy, panting. "Gotta tote it to that barrel and dump it." He pointed to a barrel some distance off. "Sometimes I git disabled to tote."

"Your Pa make you do that heavy work?" asked Judy.

"Boss man won't hire no families less'n they got boys to dip gum," said the boy. "Pa's a chipper. Me and my brother are dippers. We live in the turpentine camp over yonder."

"What's your name?" demanded Judy.

"Orrie Fletcher," said the boy.

"How d'you spell that?"

"Dunno," said the boy. "Never set foot in ary school in my life."

"You can't write your name, nor read, nor do arithmetic?" asked Joe Bob.

"Naw, can't, don't want to neither."

"How old are you?" asked Judy.

"Don't rightly know. Sometimes Ma says 'leven and agin twelve." He began to walk off through the woods.

"He don't look much bigger'n Cora Jane," said Judy. "Twelve!"

All at once Joe Bob called out after him: *"Was that your dog?"*

The boy nodded his head without looking back. Then he threw himself down full length on the ground and began to sob loud broken sobs.

Judy and Joe Bob just stood there. They felt like crying too. They stood there and watched until the boy got up and disappeared in the pines. Then they went back to the railroad track. Soon they saw some weatherbeaten shacks and a makeshift store in the middle of the woods, and near by a sprawling turpentine still.

"Betcha Orrie lives in one of them shacks," said Joe Bob.

"Reckon so," said Judy.

"Not much fun livin' in the dark, lonely woods and workin' so hard . . . and losin' your dog. . . ." said Joe Bob.

"And never goin' to school," added Judy. "That's worse'n us."

They felt a close kinship to the little turpentine worker.

"Mama told me once," said Judy, "that no matter how bad off you are, there's always some one worse off somewhere."

They kept on walking, and soon the tracks crossed the paved road.

"Here's where we turn off," said Judy.

"But where's the jalopy and the trailer . . . and the goat?" cried Joe Bob.

Judy looked in both directions and could not believe her eyes.

"Gone!" she exclaimed. "But they *can't* be, Papa's car wouldn't go." She looked at the fan belt she carried in her hand.

They walked first in one direction, then came back and walked in the other. The paved road stretched off indefinitely in both directions, but there was no sign of the jalopy.

"What'll we do?" asked Joe Bob.

"I don't know," said Judy.

They were standing by the railroad, when a large shiny car pulled up before going over the tracks. It was full of people and in the front seat sat a pretty little girl with light yellow curls. She leaned out the window and waved her hand, calling, "Hello there."

Then she added: "Why, it's Judy Drummond. What are you doing here, Judy? Mother, there's Judy. She was in my class in Florida."

All the people in the car looked at Judy and her brother standing there so stiffly.

"Is your name Judy Drummond?" called the little girl's father.

Judy gulped. "Shore is," she said. "And you're Gloria Rathbone."

She wanted to run up to the car and let Gloria know how glad she was to see a familiar face. But she remembered she had her old dirty overalls on, and her face must be dirty. She hadn't washed it since morning. She glanced at Joe Bob. His hair was wild and his face was dirty too.

"What are you doing here, Judy?" asked Gloria.

"Jest walkin' along," said Judy.

"Where are your parents?" asked Gloria.

"I don't know," said Judy.

"Can we take you to your father's car?" asked Gloria. "Has he gone off and left you? We're driving north. We spent the winter in Florida and we're on our way home to Connecticut. We'll be glad to take you, won't we, mother?"

Gloria's mother, sitting beside two other ladies, started to make space in the back. She pulled down two little folding seats.

"They can ride here," she said. "We can't leave the poor things stranded along the road. We can take them to the next town and report to the police that they are lost."

"Yes, of course," said Gloria's father. "Get in, children, we've wasted enough time already."

Gloria's mother opened the shiny back door of the car.

"How strange we should meet you children here in Georgia," she said sweetly. "Please get in, won't you?"

"No *ma'm!*" said Judy firmly. "We're stayin' here."

"Oh, won't you come with us, Judy?" begged Gloria.

But the back door of the car closed with a bang, and the car bounced softly up and down over the railroad tracks. Then it was gone, and Gloria's little hand could be seen waving good-bye out of the front window.

"Won't ride in no Yankee's car!" said Judy defiantly. To call Gloria's family Yankees gave her a strange malicious pleasure.

"Not even when they'd a took us to where Papa is?" asked Joe Bob.

"No," said Judy, "not even if I was half-dead."

"How we ever gonna find Papa?" wailed the boy.

Judy squeezed his hand tightly. She didn't know herself.

They waited a long time and finally a mule came by pulling a wagon. On the seat rode an old colored man and a little colored boy.

"Want a ride, chillen?" inquired the old man.

"Shore do," answered Judy.

Before they knew it, Judy and Joe Bob were on the wagon seat talking to Uncle Duff and little Jerry as if they had always known them. When they reached Swampville, the first thing they saw was Papa standing in front of the garage where they had been before.

They flew into his arms.

CHAPTER X

The Carolinas

L ET'S stop in beans awhile," said Mama. "Likely we can git
outdoor work here. I thought I never wanted to see another
bean, but——"

"We'll need money for gas and oil to git us to New Jersey,"
added Papa. "We'll have to stop and work somewhere."

So they stopped in South Carolina, in a small town in the
Charleston area. The farm was on the edge of town, and a railroad siding reached it from the track a mile away. Several empty
freight cars stood beside the packing shed. Papa hunted up the
grower and arranged for work. Then he set up the tent in the
shade of a tree.

Mama was feeling better and the next day she and the children walked to the bean field, while Papa went to the packing

[139]

shed to pack. They caught up with a woman and a boy who were also going to the field. The woman wore a pink flowered dress over her blue slacks, and a straw hat on her head. The boy had knee-pads on his knees.

"You-all pickin' beans?" asked Judy.

The woman frowned and spoke crossly: "Where you from?"

"We just got here from Florida," said Mama.

"You-uns can go right back where you came from," said the woman. "No more pickers needed. They use only local labor here. Plenty people here in this town need work, without out-siders comin' in."

"But the boss man hired us," said Mama.

"Crop's near about over," said the woman. "Takin' on more people ends the job for us mighty quick."

"But he said the bean crop would last till the middle of May," said Mama.

"This is the second pickin' now," said the woman. "We'll be done in less'n a week. You're takin' the bread out of our mouths." She and the boy strode on.

"*We gotta eat too!*" Judy sang out after them.

"Judy!" scolded Mama. "Hold your tongue. You only rile folks when you sass 'em back that-a-way."

The field was not as large as a Florida bean field, but it was large enough. Pickers, young and old, black and white, were scattered over it. Many of them looked like grotesque scare-crows, dressed in fantastic odds and ends of clothing. The "field walker" gave Mama two rows to pick, and Judy and Joe Bob one each. Nobody talked to them. They were left severely alone.

"Pick with two hands," said the field walker, "and fill your hands full. Keep the basket close beside you. Keep your kids with you and see that they *work*. If they stop pickin', send 'em out of the field."

He gave Mama a card to be punched each time she carried a basket to the weigher to have it weighed.

Cora Jane and Lonnie played in the dirt. Judy and Joe Bob picked. Judy wanted to help Papa all she could. It was good to be earning cash money again and she did not mind bending over at first. Then the sun grew hotter and hotter, her back began to ache and the bean row got longer and longer. But she kept on. She hoped Mama would not get sick again. Cora Jane carried a glass jar to the water tank on the truck parked at the side of the field. She brought it back full of water and they drank thirstily.

They picked beans all week, and during that time none of the other pickers spoke to them. Several truckloads of Negro families arrived from Florida, each in charge of a crew leader.

One day out in the field, Judy heard a boy's sharp scream, and saw women running.

"Somebody's hurt, I betcha," said Joe Bob.

"I'll go see if I can help," said Judy.

When Judy came up nobody spoke to her. A hoe lay on the ground with blade upturned. She guessed the boy had stumbled and fallen on the sharp blade. The women were helping him to his feet. He held his hand to his head and groaned. Blood was running down his cheek.

"Take him over in the shade," said Judy. "I'll git my First Aid kit."

"Who's she, the bossy young thing?" inquired a woman.

"Family from Florida," answered another.

The boy was taken over to the shade beside the water truck. Judy brought her kit and a wash basin which she filled with water at the tank. A large lump had risen on the boy's right temple and on top of it there was a deep cut. The women stood by not knowing what to do. A crowd of children gathered. The wounded boy, who had been standing, suddenly keeled over.

"Keep back!" said Judy. "Don't scrooge so. Can't you see he's fainted? He's gotta have air."

She looked over the crowd of children. "Here, you!" she said, choosing a little colored girl with a sober face and a kerchief tied round her head. "Take this straw hat and fan him gently." The girl dropped on her knees and began to fan. Judy bathed the boy's forehead and soon he opened his eyes again.

"Keep on fanning," said Judy to the girl.

She washed the cut out carefully and disinfected it. She nipped off adhesive and bandage just as she had seen Miss Burnette do. Then she bandaged the boy's head. When she finished, he got up, saying, "I'm O. K. now," and walked away.

Judy turned to his mother. "If he'll come to the water tank

every day at noon," she said, "I'll dress it for him and . . ."
Suddenly she gasped in astonishment. "Why, you're the woman
who . . ." She couldn't finish the sentence.

"Yes," said the woman, shamefaced. "I told you-uns to git
outa here when you first came. I said you was takin' our job
away from us. But if you hadn't come, my boy . . . well, no
tellin' what——"

"Oh, it's not a very bad cut, and I think the swelling will
soon go down," said Judy.

"I couldn't a fixed it," said the woman, "and there's no nurse
or doctor in our town." Mama came up just then. "This your
girl? She fixed my boy's head good."

Mama smiled. "Judy wants to be a nurse when she grows
up. The nurse at her school in Florida gave her that outfit
She likes to use it."

"I didn't mean it about the crop endin' so soon," said the
woman. "Course the beans is about played out, but I knew
there was potatoes comin' along. You can pick potatoes with
us. I should a told you there was plenty work for all."

"That's all right," said Mama. "If I'd a been in your place
I'd a felt the same way."

They went back to the field.

"See, Judy," said Mama, "when you're kind to people, in
stead of sassing them back, you make friends."

"Yes ma'm," said Judy.

The bean crop ended soon as the woman said it would. Th
workers moved on into a large potato field and the Drum

[144]

monds went along. The number of workers increased, but the potato field was so large it was scarcely noticeable.

The workers stooped over the rows of dead vines and gathered up the potatoes which had been loosened from the earth. They put them in baskets which they moved ahead as they picked. It was hard work and dirty work. It meant crawling on hands and knees in the dirt all day long. The Drummonds continued to pick, but every night Papa talked about starting on again. He was never contented to stay very long in one place. With a little bean and potato money in his pocket, he was anxious to drive on to pastures new.

"Call the young uns," said Mama one day. "We'll start packin' up. I need Judy to help."

It was raining and the people had been laid off at noon, but there was not a child to be seen around the shacks or packing sheds. Papa crossed the railroad siding, and hearing a murmur of voices, stopped to listen.

The voices were coming from inside one of the box-cars. Cautiously he peered round the corner. The floor had been swept clean of potato dirt and scrubbed with water. There inside stood Judy, the old Geography in one hand and a long stick in the other.

"If you young uns don't sit still, we can't have no school," she scolded.

Then Papa saw them—two rows of colored children sitting on old upturned half-bushel bean baskets. Joe Bob and Cora Jane were there too.

"What do you say when I come in?" asked Judy.

"Good morning, Teacher," they cried in chorus.

"What does the book say on the front?" asked Judy.

" '*A New World Lies Before Us*,'" answered Joe Bob promptly.

"What state are we in, Lily Belle?"

"Dunno," giggled a tall thin girl in the back row.

"Will you remember if I tell you?" asked Judy.

"Dunno," giggled Lily Belle.

"South Carolina," said Judy.

"South Ca'lina," echoed Lily Belle.

"What are the products of South Carolina?" demanded Judy. Nobody answered. Even Joe Bob didn't know.

"We doan know," said little Willie Davis. "You jest 'bliged to tell us, Teacher."

"But how should I know?" said Judy. "I don't live in South Carolina. I was born in Alabama and I been livin' in Florida."

"We come from Florida too," said several of the children.

"Likely it tells in the book," suggested the little girl who had fanned the fainting boy in the field.

Judy looked at her gratefully. "What is your name?" she asked.

"Coreena May Dickson," said the girl.

Judy leafed quickly through the Geography and found the Southern States. "It tells about North Carolina and Texas and Tennessee, but I don't see nary word about South Carolina."

She closed the book with a bang. "Well, sometimes you got to know more than the book," she said. "Now, let's us think. What do they grow right here in Charleston County?"

"Beans," answered a boy.

"POTATOES! 'TATERS!" shouted the others.

"Cabbage and cucumbers and lima beans and squash over on the island in summer time," said Lily Belle.

"Oysters—us shuck oysters," announced a boy.

"Us ketch fish and eat fish and have fish fries!"

"Us ketches fish in Four Holes Swamp," said Willie Davis.

"You does?" cried Lily Belle. "Don't you know there's ha'nts in that-ere swamp?"

"Ha'nts!" snapped Judy. "Do you-all believe in ha'nts?"

"Yes *ma'm*," chorused the local children. "Us got our doors and windows painted blue to keep the ha'nts out."

"You're plumb silly," said Judy. "Old Aunt Rilla back home on Plumtree Creek in Alabama used to try to scare us with stories of ha'nts, but my Teacher in school there told me *there ain't no ha'nts at all*!"

"Your Teacher done tole you dat?" demanded Willie Davis, wide-eyed.

"She shore did," answered Judy.

"Then it must be true," said the boy, "iffen two Teachers say so."

All this time Papa had been listening. As he slipped quietly away, Judy announced recess and the children started a game. He could hear their clear voices happily singing:

> "Here comes a girl from Baltimo'
> Balti-mo'
> Balti-mo'
> Here comes a girl from Balti-mo',
> Show us your new dress!
>
> "Bet you can't do that boo-gie
> Boo-gie
> Boo-gie
> Bet you can't do that boo-gie
> Show us your new dress!"

Papa went back and told Mama about the box-car school. As he talked he remembered Madame Rosie in Bean Town and recalled the fortune-teller's words.

"She took a fancy to Judy somehow," said Papa. "She told me to feed my young uns up and put 'em in school. Just seems like I'm no good if I can't git me a steady job so that gal can go to school regular. It makes me plumb discouraged to have them kids crawlin' on their knees and pickin' potatoes out of the dirt."

"The next crop'll be better," said Mama, "and one of these days we'll git to New Jersey."

All the colored children, including Lily Belle and Coreena May, waved goodbye when the Drummonds drove off.

"Lily Belle won't remember what state she lives in," mourned Judy, "and all those young uns will keep on believin' in ha'nts . . ."

"They won't forget what you told 'em, honey," said Papa.

"What gits ripe next?" asked Joe Bob, after South Carolina had been left behind and they had come into North Carolina. "Watermelons? I'm so hot and thirsty I could eat a big un all by myself."

"Too early in the season, son," said Papa. "Strawberries will be next, I reckon. Now that it's May, they ought to be just ripe, ready to fall off in the baskets. We'll stop and see."

But they weren't.

When they came into the strawberry area around Wilmington, they stopped to make inquiries. It was late afternoon and a man was fixing his truck by the side of the road.

"You folks berry-pickers?" asked the man.

"Yes," said Papa, "if we can find a grower to hire us."

"They won't hire you," said the man. "Better keep on goin'."

"Why's that?" asked Papa.

"Berries not ripe yet," replied the man. "Season's late on account of cold weather. A man told me they won't be ripe for three more weeks."

"Three more weeks?" gasped Mama. "What'll we live on —for three weeks? Oh, we shoulda stayed in potatoes, instead of goin' on a wild-goose chase like this—always hopin' the next crop'll be better."

"Shall we wait three weeks or keep goin' to find that next crop?" asked Papa. "We ain't got enough money to git us to Jersey."

"The grower I talked to told me he could get along with local colored people," said the man.

"I used up my last cent to git us here," said Papa. "Now there's no gas in the jalopy and no money in my pocket."

"We'll stay the night anyway," said Mama, "and think what's best to do."

"Do you know anything about this farmer?" Papa pointed to the farmhouse back at the end of the lane. "Do you reckon he'd let us camp here for the night?"

The man shrugged his shoulders. "Don't know him. I'm just passin' through. If he don't want you here, he'll run you off." He climbed into the seat of his truck and drove away.

Papa unloaded the tent while Judy milked the goat.

"Missy's not givin' much milk, Mama," said Judy. The little pail had only a cupful in it.

"No wonder with all this chasin' around," said Mama. "If Lonnie can't even have milk to drink, I don't know what we'll do. Go find a good place for Missy and stake her out for a while before dark."

Judy led the goat off to the edge of a leafy woods and staked her. The girl put her arms around the animal's neck. "You can't help it, can you, Missy?" she said. "Never gittin' no goat-chop no more. How can you make milk without good food to eat?"

Judy looked up and saw a girl about twelve years of age coming down the road with a basket of groceries. She went over to talk to her.

"You been to the store?" she asked with a friendly smile.

The girl smiled back. "Yes. Where you from?"

"We come from Florida," said Judy. "We spent our last cent for gas to git here."

"You have no money to buy food?" asked the girl.

Judy tossed her head. "Don't need none," she said. "Reckon we got some flour and fixin's left. My Papa's gonna git a job up north where they pay good wages. Do you live near here?"

"In that next house down the road there," said the girl, pointing.

Judy looked. It was a neat farmhouse with a yard and trees.

"Do you go to school?" asked Judy.

"Yes, we have good schools in North Carolina," said the girl. "The bus goes right by our house and takes us into town. I'm in Seventh Grade, next year I'll be in Eighth. What grade you in?"

Judy turned away quickly without answering. She walked

back to the tent, her shoulders hunched. Mama had put a batch of fried bread into the greasy skillet and propped it up over the smoky campfire. Mama sat on a box staring into the flames, holding sleeping Lonnie on her lap. Cora Jane was sitting on the ground.

Judy kicked the empty water bucket with her foot, and it rolled over with a clatter.

"Papa'll never git no steady job," she shouted. "He'll never git ahead. *He'll never git us a farm and I know it! I'll never git a chance to stay in one place and go to school! We'll be on the go for the rest of our days!*"

"Hold your tongue, gal!" scolded Mama. "Don't say things like that."

Just then Papa stepped into the firelight. He looked hard at Judy.

"I heard you, honey," he said. "You're mighty right. Your Papa's no good." He went inside the tent.

"Ain't you ashamed o' yourself, faultin' your Papa when he can't help it the berries ain't ripe?" said Mama. "Take that water bucket and go back up the lane to that farmer's house and git some water. Ask 'em if we can camp here tonight. Mind your manners and don't sass 'em. Hurry with the water 'cause we're thirsty and want to wash before we go to bed. Then bring the goat in and put her up for the night."

Judy took the bucket and stumbled off in the gathering dusk. When she came back with the water, it was dark. She had been gone a long time and she looked wild and disheveled.

"That cross ole man said we could camp one night," she said, "but I can't find Missy anywhere. Her rope's broke and . . ."

"Git to bed," said Mama. "You're dog-tard. The goat won't go far. We'll find her in the morning."

Early the next day Judy went for another bucket of water. Before she got to the farmhouse she could hear Missy bleating. She ran to get there quickly and saw the goat firmly chained to a fence-post in the barnyard. The farmer came out when he saw Judy.

"What d'you mean, mister, a-stealin' our goat?" demanded the girl.

The man laughed. "I'm a mind to butcher her," he said. "Roast goat's mighty tasty to eat."

Judy rushed up to the man with clenched fists. "You better not try it or I'll . . ."

"Want to know what that cussed ole goat of yours done?" asked the farmer.

"She ain't done nothin'. . ." began Judy. But she followed the man meekly.

"See that garden patch?" said the man, pointing. "She et up my garden, that's all. See them young peach trees I jest set out? She et 'em all up but the stumps. See that mock-orange bush o' my wife's? She et the top plumb off. Oh no, she ain't done nothin'!"

Judy could not believe her eyes. Her anger faded, and she began to be scared, wondering what the man would do.

"We always keep her tied up," she said in a low voice. "She broke her rope . . . she got hungry, I reckon, and had to find somethin' to eat . . . Have you ever been hungry, mister?"

The man's wife came out and was standing beside him.

"There ought to be a law agin you vagrants, roamin' around, makin' trouble for honest farmers," the man went on.

"Why don't you stay home where you belong?" asked the woman.

"Got no home!" said Judy defiantly. "Not till Papa gits a good job and a little piece of land. . . ." Then she remembered how Papa was always spending his last penny and would never get a farm, after all.

"Well, what you gonna do about all this damage?" asked the woman.

"Nothin'," answered Judy. She walked swiftly away from the farmer and his wife down the lane. Then she looked back and called out: "We ain't got a penny to pay you back. You can keep the goat for the damage she done. She'll give two quarts of milk a day if you feed her grain. But if you eat her . . . she won't taste good, 'cause she's my pet." Then she ran back to the tent as fast as she could go.

"What kept you so long?" asked Mama. "We're packin' up. We want to git goin'."

"Goin'?" gasped Judy. The word made her feel so unhappy inside, she just stood there. Three weeks to wait for the strawberries to ripen, and three weeks to pick them. *Why, she could read the Fourth Reader clear through in six weeks.* There were good schools in North Carolina, the girl who lived down the road had told her so. But they were moving on again.

"*We can't go!*" she screamed. "Papa ain't got a penny to buy gas. He said so hisself."

"He traded my sewin'-machine to a man up in town last night and got ten dollars for it," said Mama quietly. "Where's the goat?"

Judy was too stunned to answer.

"Where's Missy?" asked Mama again. "Lonnie's hungry for his milk. Go milk her."

"We ain't got no goat," said Judy dully. "I done gave her away."

CHAPTER XI

Virginia

IT WAS always good to be on the road again. Somehow, just getting into the jalopy and starting off always made the Drummonds feel they were leaving their troubles behind. It put them all in a holiday mood. Papa began to sing *You Are My Sunshine* and Joe Bob tried to whistle. Little Lonnie babbled happily.

"We'll go to Norfolk and take the ferry there," said Papa. "Up through Delaware will be the shortest route to New Jersey. Hope our tires will hold out."

"Me-eh! Me-eh! Me-e-eh!"

"Papa, I heard Missy," cried Judy.

"You couldn't. She's miles behind on that farm where you left her," said Papa.

"Me-eh! Me-e-e-eh!"

"I hear her. She's in that truck!" screamed Judy, pointing.

Papa slowed down and a truck stopped beside the car. In it sat the farmer and his wife, and over the railing in the back appeared the goat's head. The farmer opened the back of the truck and jerked the goat down.

"Take your old goat!" he shouted. "She knocked me down and nearly killed me."

"We never want to see her again," said the woman.

Judy jumped out and put her arms around Missy's neck. "So they don't want you . . . Well, we do. Joe Bob, come help me."

In a few minutes the goat was back in the two-wheeled trailer and the jalopy started on.

Route 17 was long and monotonous, running through forests of pine trees and crossing innumerable cypress swamps. It was on a long rickety bridge that Joe Bob saw the dog. He yelled so loudly that Papa stopped at once.

"What's wrong? What's happened?"

Joe Bob jumped out of the car and ran back without speaking.

"What's he after?" demanded Papa.

"A dog," said Mama, "and he'll want to keep it."

Joe Bob came up to the car carrying a small puppy in his arms. It had soft silky brown hair and big brown eyes. The children bent over to stroke it.

"It's jest a little bitty thing like Barney was," said Joe Bob, his eyes shining. "I named him after Uncle Barney—I'll name this un Barney too. He's hurt—he limps, likely a car bumped him. But there was nobody around, so he's jest a stray and nobody wants him but me."

"Git in the car," said Papa. "We can't park on a narrow bridge like this."

They rode on and came to a place where they could pull off the road and stop.

"I'll put his leg in a splint," said Judy, digging into the back of the car and bringing out her First Aid kit. "He's been scratched too—his leg's bleeding," she said.

Joe Bob found a stick and borrowed Papa's knife and whittled it. Judy put the splint on and bandaged the dog's leg.

"Oh Papa! *You'll let me keep Barney, won't you?*" cried Joe Bob. "I wouldn't mind losin' Uncle Barney's dog if I can only have this un."

"Son, you know you've forgot Uncle Barney's dog long ago," said Papa.

"No, Papa. I'll never forgit, never . . ."

"And you know we can't even buy grain for the goat, 'cause we got to save every penny for gas and oil. Do you want to keep this dog if we don't have enough food for him?"

"He'd starve all alone there on that big bridge," said the boy.

"A dog can eat a lot of food, son."

"I'll find a way," said Joe Bob. "I'll give him my own dinner."

"You can't do that, son," said Papa sternly. "We must go on now. You can keep the dog until we find some good folks to give him to—folks that will feed and take good care of him."

The boy cuddled the dog in his arms and the jalopy moved on.

It was at a roadside stand that the Drummonds met the Darnells. The Darnells hauled a home-made house-trailer behind their car. It did not take long to get acquainted. There were Mr. and Mrs. Darnell and five children—Loretta and Jenny, fourteen and twelve, Quincy and Jess, the boys, ten and eight, and little Myrtle, six.

"We been all over everywhere," said Tom Darnell, "but we started out first from Arkansas. They call us 'fruit tramps' out west. We've picked potatoes in Kansas and Minnesota, cotton in Texas and Oklahoma. In Michigan we picked cherries and apples and peaches. More cherries in Wisconsin, and tomatoes in Indiana. And oh yes, strawberries in Kentucky. We've been in over thirty-three states."

Judy brought out her Geography and she and Loretta found all the places on the map of the United States.

"How long have you been on the go?" asked Mama.

"Let's see," said Mrs. Darnell. "We started out when Loretta and Jenny were four and two—that's ten years ago. Quincy was born in cherries, Jess in cotton and Myrtle in strawberries!"

Everybody laughed.

"My, it's nice to meet you folks," said Mrs. Darnell. "We meet people from all over, at different places. We make so many friends—and then lose 'em."

"You don't git tired from bein' on the go?" asked Mama.

"Law no, we're used to it—we could never be contented stayin' all the time in one place. Now we got the house-trailer, we got our home right with us. It's easier than when you got to pack and unpack all the time."

She showed the Drummonds through the trailer. It had a tiny sitting room with pretty curtains and couches that were used for beds at night, a kitchen with sink and cupboards, and a

bedroom with double bunks each side. Judy gazed at all its wonders, speechless.

Then she listened to the men talking. Papa told about Florida and how he was planning to get work in New Jersey for the summer.

"Heard about the new cotton-picker?" asked Darnell. "They've got machines to dig potatoes and pick hops and pick corn. Next thing will be the cotton-picker."

"The tractor put the mule and the horse out of business," said Papa. "Next thing, the pickin' machines will do away with the men. I'm shore glad I ain't a cotton sharecropper—I got out jest in time."

"I used to hand-pick peas ten years ago," said Darnell. "Then that stopped and I tended a 'viner' machine which turned out more peas with two men than two hundred used to pick."

"Our pickin' days are numbered," said Papa. "I shore will have to git me that little farm and settle down."

"There's some crops the machines can't handle—yet," said Darnell. "It still takes eyes to tell when strawberries are red enough, and fingers to reach in and grab the right ones. Then there's green beans. And fruit—peaches, for instance. They need human hands. The growers can't get along without pickers—yet."

"How do you like Florida?" asked Papa.

"Sorry wages," said Darnell, "but nice place to make the winter. I been goin' up to Michigan for three-four summers now, but I thought I'd try the Atlantic coast for a change."

"Where you headin' for now?" asked Papa.

"We're jest explorin'," said Darnell. "Been thinkin' about tryin' New York State. My young uns would like to stop off in New York City and see the sights, if we go that far."

"We're goin' to New Jersey," said Papa. "Hope we'll meet up again."

They passed the Darnells several times along the road, and once they all ate a picnic supper together and camped side by side. It was there that Judy noticed Jenny's and Loretta's shoes. They were brand new. They wore new dresses too.

"We bought our shoes in Charleston with Papa's potato money," said Loretta. "Papa was foreman in a potato packing house there."

"We got our new dresses in Florida with Papa's grapefruit money," added Jenny.

"Do you wear your shoes when you go out in the field to pick?" asked Judy.

"Oh no, we pick barefooted and save our shoes for dressing up."

"Do you work or go to school?"

"Both," said Jenny. "We go to school unless it's easy picking. Or summer vacation—we pick all summer."

"I don't care how much school we miss," said Loretta. "Pop says we learn a-plenty just travelin' around."

Judy sighed happily. How nice it was to have friends again!

It was Papa who suggested that Joe Bob give the dog to

the Darnells. The dog's leg was well now and the splint and bandage had been taken off.

"Them two boys would take Barney," said Papa, "and always have plenty to feed him. Their father makes good money. They dress well and he says he's never out of a job. He's learned the tricks of this crop migration business."

"Quincy and Jess don't like Barney as much as I do," said Joe Bob.

"But they would feed him well," said Papa.

"O. K.," said Joe Bob bravely.

So the next morning when the Darnells started out, a dog sat in the front seat between Quincy and Jess.

All the way through North Carolina, Joe Bob and Judy kept their eyes open for a dusty house-trailer bouncing along behind a big old red Reo with seven people in it. Each time they stopped, they inquired, but nobody had seen it. They began to wonder if the Darnells had turned off and given up the idea of going to Norfolk.

It was late at night when they reached a small town in the Norfolk area, which had a trailer park on its outskirts. When Papa asked if he could put up his tent, the owner took him over to a tent section, and there they camped for the night.

The next morning, who should walk into the tent but Barney! He ran briskly over to the pallet bed, jumped on Joe Bob's chest and began to lick his face. Joe Bob opened his eyes and laughed. Everybody was glad to see the dog again, even Papa.

"The Darnells are in the park somewhere," cried Judy happily. "I'm going to find them."

She came back with Loretta on one arm and Jenny on the other. The house-trailer was parked only a stone's throw away. Soon Mrs. Darnell strolled over to see Mama.

"They're havin' Sunday meetin' out under the trees," she said. "Don't you folks want to come with us? It's mostly for the young uns, they give 'em story papers to keep, but there's prayin' and preachin' and singin'——"

"Oh Mama," cried Judy, "just what you been wishin' for ever since Florida!"

"Bless goodness!" exclaimed Mama, astonished. "Here, in a trailer camp, right under the trees, without no meetin'-house?"

"Sure," said Mrs. Darnell. "A preacher comes here every week, they tell me. They have meetin' for the migrants in lots of camps in California, and in the Middle West too. It's for everybody—it don't matter what church you belong to."

"But what'll I wear?" wailed Mama. "I ain't been to meetin' since we left Plumtree Creek."

Mama's old Sunday dress was badly mussed and so was Judy's feed-sack dress, but nobody noticed. They all went to the inter-faith service and sat on plank benches in the shade. There were all kinds of other people there. The preacher played a portable organ and when they sang *What a Friend We Have in Jesus,* the tears rolled down Mama's face.

But Judy did not cry—she was too happy. Her happiness lighted up her face as she listened to the music and all the things the preacher said. His text was *Do Unto Others,* and he talked about how to get along with strangers. One thing he said, Judy remembered: "There's only one way—be kind to others *first.* Don't wait for them to be kind to you."

While they were singing *Shall We Gather at the River,* Barney jumped out of Quincy Darnell's arms and ran up to the front and barked at the organ. Everybody laughed as Joe Bob ran to pick him up. As the meeting closed, the people were friendly and stayed and talked together. Each of the children was given a different story paper, so Judy spent the rest of the day reading stories aloud to the little ones.

On Monday morning Tom Darnell came to take Papa away and see about jobs for both families. When the men returned, they said there was work for everybody. Papa laughed and said his luck had turned, but Mama and Judy knew it was because Tom Darnell put new life in him by his energetic example.

"Papa, can I keep Barney?" begged Joe Bob, holding the dog up in his arms. "The boys say I can have him again."

"You shore can, son," said Papa, "now I've got me a good job."

They all stayed in Virginia for two months, May and June.

Strawberries were ripe first. The men worked in the packing sheds and everybody else went out in the field to pick. The grower had truckloads of pickers brought out every day from Norfolk, crowds of Negro families. He also sent a truck to the trailer camp to transport the workers there. The road back and forth to the fields was very rough, so the two families decided to save gas and tires by riding in the grower's truck. It was always so crowded with pickers, they had to ride standing.

They had great fun picking. They laughed and joked as they filled the baskets. They ran races to see who could pick the most in the shortest time. Loretta always won. Her fingers were nimble from years of experience. At eleven each morning the picking stopped, so the berries could be shipped before night. The rest of the day the children played.

Strawberries lasted three weeks, then beans came on, but beans were a different story. The crop of beans was heavy and the rows were long. The Darnell children were experienced pickers, and try as hard as she could, Judy always fell behind. Joe Bob got tired by noon and skipped off in the shade of a woods near by, to play with his dog.

But potatoes, which followed beans, were the worst of all. It meant crawling all day long in the dirt, as they had done back in South Carolina. After a week, Mrs. Drummond had to stop. She stayed at the tent and cooked the meals, keeping Cora Jane and Lonnie and Myrtle Darnell with her. Judy was the only Drummond left in the field.

She thought of Loretta's and Jenny's new shoes, and of the Darnells' house-trailer. Tom Darnell had four children and his wife, all experienced pickers, to help him. He himself was a big strong man, twice the size of Jim Drummond. It was easy to see why he got ahead so much better than Papa did.

If only Joe Bob would help more, but all he wanted to do was play with his dog. And Mama had to stop picking so she would not get sick again. Papa had only Judy to help him.

Potatoes—potatoes—nothing but potatoes. Judy was sicker of potatoes than she had been of beans. The sun got hotter and hotter. Her ragged overalls stuck to her, and she was red with sunburn and prickly heat. Her straw hat made her head too hot, so she tossed it off. Her back ached badly—she must rest for a minute. She stretched out full length in the dirt.

Lying there, Judy remembered her Geography. School had faded away. She could hardly recall her teacher at Plumtree Creek or Miss Norris at Bean Town. Long ago in Alabama, Papa had bragged that his children were not going to pick, they were going to school to learn things. She had finished the Third Reader . . . or was it the Fourth. . . . She tried to remember.

She raised her head and saw that she was being left behind. The Darnells were always ahead in their rows. She roused herself and began to pick up potatoes again. There was no one else to help Papa.

Potatoes, sun and dirt. Potatoes, sun and dirt. But when the day ended, there would be a bath . . . plenty of water at the trailer camp . . . a tap of running water. . . . She didn't have to wash in the molasses bucket the way she did at Bean Town. They could have all the water they wanted without paying a nickel a bucketful, as people had to do in some places. She would sit in the washtub and Mama would pour several bucketfuls over her for a shower when she got back. How good it would feel!

She kept on putting the potatoes into the basket. She shoved the basket along—it was too heavy to lift.

Then she heard the field walker's whistle.

The end of the day had come at last. The baskets were loaded and the pickers hurried to the trucks. The driver of the truck for the trailer camp honked his horn. Judy was the last one to get on. There was no place to sit down, and there was no tail-board on the truck. She clung tightly to the side, as the truck started off down the rough, bumpy road.

About halfway back to the camp, loud screams rang out. Over the noise of the engine and the rattle of the truck the

driver heard, and put on his brakes. The truck stopped so abruptly, most of the pickers were thrown off their feet.

"Oh, the poor child!" cried Mrs. Darnell.

There in the dusty road lay Judy, thrown from the truck. Her face was deathly white and her eyes were closed.

Mrs. Darnell reached her first. The other pickers jumped down and crowded round. Joe Bob looked on with a scared, drawn face. The woman examined the girl carefully and saw that no bones were broken. Judy opened her eyes.

"Help me lift her, you," said Mrs. Darnell to the driver. "Get those big boys out of the front seat. I'll take her in there with me."

The driver helped to lift Judy, and Mrs. Darnell climbed up. "If you'd a had a tail-board on your truck, this wouldn't a happened."

" 'Tain't my truck," said the driver. "Belongs to the boss."

"Poor kid," said Mrs. Darnell. "The sun's been too much for her. She's half starved too—hasn't had proper food for a coon's age. The whole family work their heads off, but they're poor, dirt poor."

The truck bounced on again.

Everybody called it sunstroke. Judy had to stay in bed for a week. The driver reported the accident to the boss, and a tail-board was put on the truck. The boss came around and was relieved when he learned that the girl had not been seriously injured and need not go to the hospital.

One afternoon when Judy woke up from a brief nap, she

had a surprise. A pair of black shiny shoes sat on the box beside her pallet bed. She looked at them listlessly.

"Papa shouldn't pay cash money for shoes," she said. "We want to save up for a farm."

"Papa didn't buy 'em," said Mama. "They're a present from the Darnells."

"Guess we don't need their ole presents," said Judy. "We're makin' out by ourselves. We're makin' out fine. When can I go back to the field?"

"You can't go," said Mama. "Potato crop's over. Job's over. We're movin' on."

Judy did not pick up the shoes or touch them.

Shoes! New shoes! She remembered the two Welfare ladies in Florida and how she had expected them to bring shoes. You had to have shoes before you could go to a birthday party. How did the Darnells know what size to get? *What if the shoes were not the right size?*

"Don't believe she wanted 'em, after all," Mama whispered to Mrs. Darnell outside the tent. "She ain't had shoes for years now, she don't hardly know what they're for, poor young un."

"She don't like 'em?" exclaimed Loretta and Jenny, disappointed.

"Let her rest, she's not herself," said Mama.

After a while Joe Bob peeped into the tent. He came back, his eyes shining.

"She's pattin' them shoes with her hand, the way I pat Barney," he said. "She likes 'em all right."

[170]

CHAPTER XII

Delaware

"You are my sunshine,
My only sunshine,
You make me happy
When skies are gray.
You'll never know, dear,
How much I love you,
Please don't take
My sunshine away . . ."

OH, STOP your singin', Judy," said Joe Bob. "I'm tard o' your singin' and I'm tard o' ridin'. Won't we never git nowheres?"

"Purty soon, son," said Papa. He hummed the tune of Judy's song contentedly.

It seemed weeks since the Drummonds had put the jalopy on the ferry across Chesapeake Bay to Cape Charles. There was nothing to be harvested in Maryland but potatoes, so Papa would not stop. Whenever he thought of potatoes, he remembered Judy's accident. He followed Route 13 on and on northward into Delaware. There a county agent told Papa of a grower who was hiring pickers for his apple and peach crops. He had a large orchard of thousands of trees and his early summer apples were ready for harvesting in July. Scores of pickers, black and white, native and foreign, women and children, were taken to the orchards each day.

Tony Torresina, the foreman, lived in a farmhouse a short distance from one of the orchards. A small building, formerly used for a chicken coop, had been simply furnished, and Tony told the Drummonds to move in.

"It's better than the tent," said Mama.

"It's got a floor and four walls and a roof," said Judy.

While they were unpacking, a large, fat, smiling woman bustled out of the farmhouse, with several black-haired children hanging to her skirts. Her words had a strange accent which the Drummonds had never heard before, but her tone and her actions were friendly. She helped Mama unpack and get things settled.

"You gotta de goat, eh?" chuckled Mrs. Torresina. "Goin' dry, eh? Well, we take good care of her. We like-a de goat and de goat's milk, it good for bambina."

Mama asked about water.

Mrs. Torresina pointed to the house. "Your kids—they take turns bringin' the water, yes? Angie show you where is the pump. Angie! Angel-*eena*! Angel-*eena*!"

A girl of Judy's age came running out of the farmhouse. She wore a red blouse and a bright blue skirt. She had striped socks on her legs and red sneakers on her feet. Her black hair curled loosely on her shoulders. Her black eyes sparkled as she smiled.

Judy stared. She had never seen a girl like her before.

"Show her where is the pump, Angie," said Mrs. Torresina. "Go pump water for her."

Judy picked up the water bucket and walked stiffly at the girl's side, now and then glancing at her out of the corner of her eye. Her mind was made up. She was not going to make any more new friends. Traveling like this, when you made friends, you always had to give them up and never see them again.

The Darnells were gone. She had loved Loretta and Jenny so much. They had given her the new shoes, the new shoes she had never worn. Their father had helped Papa get the best job he ever had, which had put a nice nest-egg into Mama's stocking at last. But the Darnells had decided to go west into the Shenandoah Valley. When they said goodbye, they promised to meet the Drummonds in Florida next winter, but Judy knew she would never see the girls again.

She turned to the Italian girl and asked suddenly, "Is this *up north?*"

The girl was puzzled. "Oh, *north,* yes, up there." She pointed straight ahead.

"Are you a Yankee?" asked Judy.

"Yan-kee, what's that?" asked Angelina. "No, I'm a gypsy! Gypsy Angie they call me. You know what a gypsy is?"

Judy shook her head.

"I put earrings in my ears—see the holes?" She pointed to her ears and Judy stared. "I got a tambourine with bells on it, and I dance and play and sing. I wear sneakers so I can dance and climb ladders and pick apples. . . . You don't know what a tambourine is? Or a gypsy?"

Each girl seemed to be talking a strange language to the other.

"Your Grandpa was a Yankee then," insisted Judy. "He was a soldier and he came south and he stole all the cattle and silver and . . ."

Angelina's smile faded. "My Grampa he never steal nothing," she said. "He live in Italy, he grow grapes on the hillside, my Mama tell me. We send-a him money to come to this country, but he die there and he can't come."

"Oh . . ." said Judy, taken aback.

Suddenly she remembered Patrick Joseph Timothy Mulligan, the old Irishman who had been Joe Bob's fishing companion on the canal bank in Florida. He was born in Killarney, Ireland, and she had found it on the map.

"If your Grandpa was born and died in Italy," she said slowly, "then he couldn't a been a soldier in the War Between the States."

"No," said Angelina patiently. "He grew grapes and made wine. I never heard of no War Between the States."

"No?" For the first time Judy realized there were many people who had come to the United States after the Civil War, so they knew nothing of it.

"Do you go to school?" asked Judy.

"In wintertime, yes," said Angelina. "Not now—it summer, it vacation. We have a good time, yes?"

Judy smiled. They pumped the water and took the bucket back to the chicken coop. Then Angelina went in the house and came out with something wrapped in paper.

"We go to the orchard, yes?" coaxed Angelina.

The young trees were planted in straight rows and were covered with red-cheeked fruit. Angelina handed Judy an apple. She bit into it deeply. She had never tasted an apple before.

"You like it, eh?" The girl waited, smiling.

"Oooh yes," said Judy. "It's *good*."

"You never had apples before, to eat?"

"No, but we had oranges in Florida," said Judy, her mouth full. "They grow on trees in a grove, and you're not supposed to pick 'em. Sometimes they drop on the ground . . ."

"Just like apples in Delaware," said Angelina. "But we say 'orchard' not 'grove.' "

" 'Orchard!' How funny!" laughed Judy, biting close to the apple's core. "I used to think a tree full of oranges was the most beautiful thing in the world, but now, a tree full of red apples . . . is beautiful too. Tell me your name again."

"Angelina Torresina," said the girl. "Now eat this." She opened the paper parcel and stuffed a fat bologna-cheese sandwich into Judy's mouth. It was so big Judy had to hold it with two hands. Angelina ate a second sandwich herself.

"You like it—the grub? It make-a you fat—the grub?"

Judy nodded her head. She could not speak.

"Angie! Angel-eena!" came a call from the distance.

"My mother, she is calling. Come, let's go," said Angelina.

They took hands and ran through the orchard. That was the

first of many happy days there. Mama and Mrs. Torresina also became good friends.

"We lived in Philadelphia," said Mrs. Torresina. "My man, he had a good trade, he make-a de back pockets for men's pants in a factory, but he not like it. Every spring, the padrone he come from New Jersey to get-a de pickers to work in the crops in the summer. Yes, we make-a de beeg money. We come in de truck and we work all summer in de fields and go back to de city when school begins. But we not like it. In de city, all de houses so close together, we packed like-a de sardine in de box. You no can breathe, you no can sleep for de noise, you no can see de sky. The kids—no place to play but in de street. You never live in beeg city, no?"

"No," said Mama.

"So we come to de country to live," Mrs. Torresina went on, "and my man, he get-a de job here. We like it better, where is a little fresh air to blow. We got a beeg house to live in, beeg eats and beeg money!"

Every day the Drummond family went into the orchard with the Torresinas. Papa and Mama and Mrs. Torresina picked by the hour, wearing baskets fastened over the right shoulder and under the left arm. Judy and Angelina picked too, and even Joe Bob liked to climb the ladders, while the little children played on the ground.

"Oooh, I'm highest!" cried Judy, looking over the top of the tree to see Angelina. They laughed and talked to each other, but when they laughed too much, Angelina scolded.

"You want to fall and break-a your neck?" she cried. "We not laugh now, we not talk. We not say one word till we get our baskets full."

So for a while they picked and only looked at each other. Then the talking and laughing would begin again. Judy loved being with Angelina because there was never a dull moment.

On the last day of the apple picking, the Torresinas brought a big picnic dinner to the orchard, and after everybody had eaten, Angelina played her tambourine and danced her gypsy dance in the shade of an apple tree. She had put her mother's gold band earrings in her ears, and she danced and whirled to the rhythm of the music. When she dropped breathless on the grass, they all clapped. Judy thought Angelina was the most beautiful girl in the world.

After the early apples were picked, they moved into the peach orchard. Here the trees were lower, and most of the picking could be done from the ground. On certain days, the women worked in the packing house, getting the peaches ready for shipment.

One Saturday afternoon Papa took the family in to the nearest town. It was an important occasion. Judy wore her feedsack dress and her new shoes. Sitting in the car she kept looking at them, admiring their shininess. *I shall wear them all day today because they are new,* she thought. But when she got out on the sidewalk, it seemed strange to walk in them.

The town was crowded with people and cars. They had to park a long way out and walk back to the stores. Papa had money in his pocket to spend, so they all went to the dime store, which sold things for a dime and up. Mama bought new dresses for herself and for the girls, a new suit for Lonnie, and new shirts and overalls for Joe Bob and Papa. It took a long time to buy everything, and Judy's shoes began to pinch her feet.

"I'll go to the car and take my shoes off," she whispered to Mama.

"Take the young uns out with you and wait at the corner," said Mama. "Then we'll go to the shoe store and git 'em sneakers. They can't have real shoes like yours—not just yet."

The children waited patiently on the street corner. Lonnie and Cora Jane had colds and their noses were running. Joe Bob begged for an ice-cream cone. Judy's shoes hurt her feet. The words of the old colored woman back in Georgia came to her: *Shoes is a heavy cross to bear.*

She wiped Lonnie's and Cora Jane's noses on her skirt. She told Joe Bob to wait till Papa came. Then she could stand the new shoes no longer. *Lawsy, my feetses hurts from walkin' so fur. Soon as I gits home, I's gonna take off my shoes and rest my feetses good.* Judy could still hear the old woman's voice. Wasn't it strange how things that happened to you became a part of you . . . you could never forget them . . . *I won't wait till I git home,* she decided. She sat down on the curbstone and took her shoes off.

People who passed stared at the little group. A crowd of children began to gather in front of the movie theater. They stood in line to buy tickets, but the window was not open yet.

"White trash!" said one boy, pointing to the children at the curb.

Judy paid no attention.

"Hillbillies from Tennessee, I betcha!" cried another boy.

Judy thought of the Holloways who had told them about work in New Jersey. Would she ever see Tessie again?

"They haven't any money. They can't go to the movies like us," said a big girl in the line.

"Reckon we can go if we *want* to," answered Judy.

She stood up, her new shoes firmly clenched in her hand. She hadn't felt so angry since that day in the Florida school when the Cracker children had called her and Bessie names.

"They never wash their faces!" said the big girl.

"They never comb their hair," added another.

"Look—their dresses aren't even ironed," said a third.

"We're as clean as you are," Judy answered in a low voice.

"Look at their dirty feet, but say, the big girl's got *new shoes*!" teased the first boy. "She wears them on her hands!"

All the children in the line laughed.

Judy remembered her pride and joy in her new shoes. She wouldn't let these town-kids spoil it. She wished she had apples or peaches in her hands instead of the shoes, so she could throw them. Then she saw Joe Bob advancing with his fist doubled up.

"You let my sister alone," yelled Joe Bob.

Without stopping to think, Judy dropped her shoes and

joined him. A fight began. Judy hit at the big girl and Joe Bob jumped on the boy and threw him. The children in the line scattered and the young woman in the glassed-in ticket office screamed, but nobody could hear her. A few people looked on, smiling. Then a policeman appeared.

"What's this?" he asked. "Cats and dogs fightin', eh?"

"They called us names," screamed Judy, "so we beat 'em up! They think 'cause they live in a town and go to the movies . . . We'll beat 'em up, we'll . . ."

"Now, now, no need o' that," said the policeman. He pulled out his stick. "I'm the one who does the beatin' up. Any time you need help, just call on me." He pulled Judy away from the girl and jerked Joe Bob to his feet.

Frowning, Judy looked out from under her tousled hair and breathed hard. At that moment she hated the whole world.

The children formed in line again. The door of the movie theater opened. Adults began going in. The children followed, the fighting boy and girl among them.

It was true what they had said. Judy and her brothers and sister could not go to the movies. There wasn't money enough. She turned around. Joe Bob sat on the curb nursing a black, swollen eye. Cora Jane and Lonnie were crying. Then Judy remembered.

"*Where are my new shoes?*" she demanded.

"I dunno . . ." wailed Cora Jane.

"Stop bawling and tell me," said Judy. "I gave them to you to hold."

"You never . . . you never . . ." insisted Cora Jane.

Judy looked all over the sidewalk and gutter, but the shoes were nowhere to be seen. She sat down on the curb with a thump.

"Sticks and stones can break my bones, but words can never hurt me." The old saying rang through her mind. *Oh if I'd a been nice to them kids, I'd a still had my shoes. But I was mean. I never stopped to think. I sassed 'em back. My hot tongue always gits me in trouble, like Madame Rosie said. I fought them kids and beat 'em up. That's why I lost my shoes . . ."*

"Is something the matter?"

Judy looked up and saw a nicely dressed girl standing beside her.

"Where do you live?" asked the girl. "Where's your home?"

"Ain't got none," blurted out Judy.

"Come to my house then and get washed up," said the girl. "I saw the fight and I know you are in trouble."

"We're used to trouble," sniffed Judy. "We're always in trouble."

The girl took her by the hand, and the children followed. They all walked down a side street and soon came to a pretty house set back in a yard behind a fence. There were flowers blooming beside the path.

Judy looked. The house was very familiar—she felt as if she had seen it before. Then she remembered. It was that dream house that Madame Rosie had talked about, that always lived in the back of her mind.

"Is this a picket fence?" she asked.

"Yes," said the girl. "My name is Barbara Delmar. I live here. Come in and see my house. My mother's away, but she'll be back soon. She gave me money to go to the show, but I'm tired of shows and I saw you and . . . I knew you needed a friend."

Judy did not know what to say. She and the children walked through the house slowly, looking at everything. It was the first time they had been inside a real house since they had left the Gibsons'. The floors had carpets, the walls had pretty wallpaper and were hung with pictures. The windows had white curtains with ruffles. The house was clean and orderly.

Barbara took the children into a shiny bathroom to wash up. She had to turn the water on and off. They had never been in a bathroom before and did not know how.

"Now, let's eat some ice cream." Barbara went to an electric icebox and dished out dishes of pink and white ice cream. The children sat down and ate silently and slowly. Then they got up to go.

"You haven't told me your name yet," said Barbara.

"Judy Drummond," answered Judy. She told Barbara the children's names too. "We live in a chicken coop out at . . ."

"It's not the chicken coop that's important," said Barbara, "but *how* you live in it. . . ."

Judy nodded. "Papa's got a good job now, and some day we're goin' to have a farm of our own."

"Come and see me again, Judy," said Barbara.

[185]

They trailed out the gate.

Barbara's friendliness eased the bitterness and pain in Judy's heart. When they got back to the corner where the movie theater was, she looked again for her shoes, but they were not there. Somebody must have picked them up. The same policeman was busy directing traffic.

Papa and Mama appeared. "We've been lookin' high and low for you," said Mama. "Where you been?"

Judy told about the fight and the loss of her shoes. "Them kids was mean," she growled. "They said mean things."

"People are what you think they are," said Papa. "If you think they're good and treat 'em right, they'll *be* good and treat *you* right. But first, you got to be plumb good your own self." He turned to Mama. "Buy her some sneakers."

The loss of the shoes she had worn only once faded away in new happiness over the unexpected sneakers. Judy could hardly wait to get back home.

"Angie! Angel-*eena*!" she called. She pointed to her feet. "Red sneakers like yours!"

"Good!" said Angelina, smiling.

CHAPTER XIII

New Jersey

ONWARD, still going *up north,* the old jalopy rolled along, with the two-wheeled trailer bouncing behind and Missy bleating noisily. Apples and peaches were over in Delaware and the Drummonds were headed for New Jersey. It was the last week of August.

Through Delaware, they followed route 13 to New Castle. A short ferry ride across Delaware Bay and they were in New Jersey at last.

"Will there be school, Papa?" asked Judy.

"I hope so, honey," said Papa. "But first we'll see what crops we can find. Holloway told me to go to Cumberland County and I'd find work a-plenty."

"Do you reckon we'll see Tessie and Gwyn?" asked Judy.

"They're in New Jersey somewhere," said Papa, "but it's not likely we'll run into 'em."

Once again Judy had had to part with a friend—happy, carefree, good-natured Angelina. She tried not to think of her any more. She tried to remember what Tessie Holloway was like. Would she know her if she saw her again?

"Is this *up north?*" demanded Joe Bob.

"I reckon it is," said Papa, laughing. "It's New Jersey."

"But it's not cold enough," said Joe Bob.

"It's hot summer now," said Papa.

"But I thought they had snow up north," insisted Joe Bob.

"Not till winter, boy." They all laughed.

Papa stopped to see the County Agent who sent him out to the Simpson Company, a cannery and packing house three miles from town. Mama got a job peeling tomatoes and Papa a general job in the plant. They were to live in a dormitory camp owned by the company. Long barracks were divided into two-room apartments, which were furnished with two beds, a bureau, table, stove, and boxes for chairs. Other families from Tennessee and West Virginia were their neighbors. Mrs. Tyler from the end apartment, came in to greet them and get acquainted.

Judy inquired for the Holloways, but no one had heard of them. There were no other children in camp, but Judy learned that the school bus passed by every day.

Eagerly Judy waited for the opening of school.

A truck called at the camp before six every morning to take

Mama and Papa and the other workers to the plant, so Judy had everything to do at home. She washed the children's clothes and borrowed Mrs. Tyler's iron, to iron them. She was glad when Mrs. Tyler, who was not working, offered to keep Lonnie during school hours.

Labor Day passed and the first day of school came.

Judy dressed the children, washed them and combed their hair, and gave them breakfast. Then she staked the goat out in a bushy field. The children stood out by the side of the road for half an hour before the bus came along.

That afternoon, Judy came running in from the bus, eager to tell Mama all about the first day of school. But the dormitory was bleak and empty. Mama was at the plant and had to work until six. There was supper to get.

Judy went over to Mrs. Tyler's. Little Lonnie met her at the door, crying hard.

"I got bad news for you," said Mrs. Tyler. "Your mother's been taken to the hospital. She got sick at the plant. She should never have started working. She won't be home for a few days."

Judy's world suddenly began to whirl. School! School! Only one day, and now already it was over. She sat down on the bed, sick at heart. She couldn't expect Mrs. Tyler to keep Lonnie every day. She would have to stay home and look after him. She would keep Cora Jane home too, like the teacher said, until she got over her cold. She would have to cook all the meals. She dragged Lonnie back to the dormitory.

"How was school?" asked Papa when he came.

"I got a real nice teacher, Miss Billings," said Judy. "In our class we can go just as fast as we're able to. I'll bring my books home and study here till Mama gets well again."

"Too bad, honey," said Papa. "Seems like there's always somethin' to keep you outa school."

"Papa, you got cash money for the doctor and medicines?" asked Judy.

"Now, sugarpie, don't you worry," laughed Papa. "Don't you recollect that little nest-egg in Mama's stockin'? And here we are in a dry house with a floor and everything. Ain't we the lucky ones?"

"Papa, what'll we do when it snows?" asked Judy.

"Make snowballs and throw 'em like cotton," laughed Joe Bob.

"Papa," Judy went on, "if it gits cold, I'll have to git a new coat to wear to school, and some stockin's."

"Me too," said Joe Bob.

"Me too," echoed Cora Jane and Lonnie.

"Lucky I got a good job," said Papa. "Beeg money, like Mrs. Torresina used to say. Enough to pay for everything!"

"Can we start payin' for our farm?" asked Judy. "Is it beeg enough for that?"

"Honey, when this job's over, how would you like to go south again and hunt for that little farm?"

"Oh Papa!" Judy threw her arms around him. "Oh Papa!" She couldn't find any other words to say.

It seemed very lonely with Mama away. Papa bought groceries and Judy cooked the meals as well as she could. Mrs. Tyler sometimes sent over an appetizing dish to help out, and on the days when she offered to keep Lonnie, Judy went to school.

It was the strangest school that Judy had ever been in, and after a few days, she thought it was the nicest. She and Joe Bob and Cora Jane were all in the same class—a special class for migrant children, who ranged in age from six to thirteen. Some as old as ten or eleven had never been in school before. There were Southern Negro, Japanese-American, and mountain children from Tennessee and West Virginia, besides New Jersey children, some of foreign descent. Each child was allowed to advance at his own pace until he was ready to be placed in the regular grades.

One day in the playground, a little colored girl had a fall and the other children crowded round. Judy ran to see. The girl was not hurt, but her nose was bleeding badly.

"Look! Blood!" cried the children. "It makes me sick to see blood," said one. "I'm scared, I wouldn't touch her," said another.

"Don't be silly," said Judy. "I'm not afraid of blood. I'm going to be a nurse."

"Are you?" asked the little girl. "So'm I."

Judy cleared a place on the steps and asked the girl to lie down. She bunched her sweater up under her neck, to tip her head back. Judy wished she could remember what the First Aid booklet said to do for nosebleed. "Wisht I had my First

Aid kit," she said. "We'll have to have water and a cloth."

"Miiko's bringing them," cried the children.

"Here they are." A little Japanese-American girl with short bobbed hair and slanting eyes brought a basin of water and held it out. A towel hung over her arm.

"Thank you, Miiko," said Judy.

Judy washed the blood off the girl's face, then wrung the towel out of water and laid it across her forehead. It was not long before she was able to be on her feet again.

"You feel-a better?" asked Rosa Maria, a little Italian girl who looked and spoke like Angelina.

"Good as new," said the colored girl, getting to her feet.

Judy looked at her more closely. "Haven't I seen you before . . ? Why, you're the girl who fanned that boy who fell on the hoe. Let's see, that was back in . . ."

"South Carolina," added the girl. "I'm Coreena May Dickson."

"Oh, Coreena May, now I remember. How did you get up here?" asked Judy.

"Our crew leader brought us to pick beans," said Coreena May. "We been here since July. I picked beans all summer. I can pick twenty hampers a day."

"I never picked more than fifteen," confessed Judy. "Where do you live, Coreena May?"

"At Oak Tree Camp," said the girl, "about six miles from here. We're goin' back to Florida soon. Are you?"

Judy frowned. "Not yet. I like school, I want to stay in school . . ."

"I watched the way you bandaged that boy's head," said Coreena May. "That gave me the idea of being a nurse too. So I thought I better come to school every chance I git. I ain't forgot the school in the box-car . . ."

"It was better than no school at all," laughed Judy.

It was Coreena May who told Miss Billings about it. So Judy brought her old worn Geography to school the next day and all the children looked at the maps and found the places where their families had come from.

Then Miss Billings asked Judy to tell the class about her travels.

Judy felt very shy until she realized she had something to say that the children wanted to hear. She stood up in front of the class and talked about her travels from Alabama to New Jersey. She showed the class all the places she had been on the map and mentioned the crops raised there. She ended up by telling about the little farm her father was going to get.

All the children clapped and Miss Billings said, "You may have missed a good bit of school, Judy, but you have gained a good background of information from your travel and work experiences." She called upon the children for comments.

"I liked the things Judy told us," said Ramon, a Mexican boy.

"I am glad that Judy is in our class," said Miiko.

"Judy was my friend in South Carolina," said Coreena May, "and now she is my friend in New Jersey."

"We are all glad that Judy is in our class, aren't we, children?" said Miss Billings.

"Yes, yes," answered the children.

Nothing so important had ever happened to Judy before. She had had no praise in her life. She had never been publicly praised in school. She could hardly wait to get home to tell Mama about it. The children had not called her names or said she was dirty or made fun of her clothes. *They were glad to have her in their class.* She had contributed something to the group. When she got off the bus, she ran all the way to the dormitory and . . . then she remembered. Mama was not there. Mama was still sick at the hospital.

She stopped at the Tylers' for Lonnie, but neither he nor Mrs. Tyler was there. So she and Joe Bob and Cora Jane played with Barney for a while. Judy put off going home as long as possible, but at last she said, "I must go start supper."

As she ran across the yard, with the children at her heels, she heard voices talking and laughing. When she opened the door, a surprise met her eyes.

The first thing she saw was Mama, back again from the hospital, sitting up in bed. Papa was there too, and Mrs. Tyler had supper started on the stove. A pot of beef stew was cooking. The four children stood still and looked. Mama was well again, and there was the new baby in her arms.

"Oh Mama! Oh Mama!" they cried.

"Come and see your new little sister," said Mama. "I've named her Jersiana." They all crowded round.

And then Judy saw the Holloways—Tessie and Gwyn and their baby and their parents. She would have known Tessie

anywhere. The next minute she was in Tessie's arms, and everybody was talking at once. The Holloways had been working for another New Jersey grower, but had come to the Simpson Company and had now moved into an apartment at the other end of the same dormitory. The Holloways were to be neighbors again.

After that, Tessie and Gwyn went on the same bus to school every morning, and were in the same class with the Drummond children.

Judy told all the children at school about the new baby, and one day Miss Billings brought a group of them out to see her. She brought Miiko from California and Ramon from Mexico and Coreena May from South Carolina and Rosa Maria from Philadelphia and Charles from Texas and Shirley from West Virginia and Jeanette from Tennessee.

As Mama grew stronger, she found that working in the plant were people of different races and from different localities in this country. A group of women came to see her and brought a complete outfit of clothes and bedding for the new baby. It made Mama so happy she cried. Nothing like this had ever happened to her before. She was surprised to learn that she had so many friends.

One Saturday afternoon, Judy went to town with Papa. After doing their shopping, Papa took Judy to a carnival being held in the baseball park and bought her a double ice-cream cone. They looked at the bingo counters, shooting galleries and wheels of chance, then had a ride on the Ferris wheel. When they got off, there in front of them they saw a tent with the sign: MADAME ROSIE—PALM READINGS—SPEAKS SEVEN LANGUAGES, and there was Madame Rosie herself. She grabbed hold of Papa's arm.

"You made any money, mister?" she demanded. "You gettin' that house for this little girl? You been feedin' her up a little better?"

Papa explained about his good job and the new second-hand car he was going to get to take the place of the jalopy.

"Don't spend your money on a car, save it for that house," said the fortune-teller.

"Maybe I better," said Papa thoughtfully.

"Did I stiffen your backbone for you?" asked Madame Rosie, laughing.

"You shore did," laughed Papa. "You near about scared the life outa me. But *why?*"

"I'll tell you a secret," said Madame Rosie. "I was afraid Judy's fortune would never come true. We fortune-tellers just say nice things to people—whatever they want to hear. Sometimes maybe it helps 'em, I don't know. Sometimes we just say anything to get their money—we got to live, too. I just wanted your girl to have a decent home to live in. I wanted it for her, bad, so I tried to——"

"You helped," said Papa. "We're startin' to Florida soon, and we're aimin' to git us a farm and a house."

"And a mule and a cow and a cat," added Judy. "Joe Bob's got his dog."

Madame Rosie said, "Wait a minute," and disappeared inside her tent. When she came out, she brought a string of bright blue glass beads—the same color as Pinky Jenkins' blue bottle—and dropped them around Judy's neck. Then she bent down and kissed her on each cheek.

"Good luck!" she said softly. "And everything that goes with it—health, happiness and prosperity."

"What a woman!" said Papa, as they walked away. "A mountain of a woman."

"She was the first friend I made after I left Plumtree Creek," said Judy.

"And a real one too," said Papa.

The tomato and lima bean season lasted well into October, but it was November before the doctor said Mama was strong enough to travel. Papa decided to take Madame Rosie's advice and not spend money on another car, because he would need a truck in Florida if he bought a farm. He got out the old jalopy and began to collect new "parts" for it, to get it in shape for the long trip south.

"The ducks are going," laughed Papa. "Time for us to start."

"But Papa," said Joe Bob, "I haven't seen snow. I thought we came *up north to see snow.*"

"Oh Papa," cried Judy, "I'm finishing the Fourth Reader. Soon I can go into the regular Fifth Grade, Miss Billings says. How can I leave Rosa Maria and Tessie and Shirley and Miiko and Coreena May?"

"You-all jest want to stay *up north and be Yankees,* I see that!" teased Papa.

All the neighbors in the dormitory came in the night before the Drummonds left. They visited and talked and played games, and there were refreshments for all.

The next morning Papa routed the family out early. It was just daylight and the sky looked dark and heavy when they climbed into the old jalopy. Joe Bob brought Barney on a leash and Papa went to bring Missy from her shed in the yard behind the dormitory.

"Looky here," he called out. "We've got two extra passengers to take along with us."

The children went around behind the car. There stood two wobbly kids, one black and one white. Missy was bleating proudly as she nuzzled them. Papa loaded them carefully into the trailer.

"Oh Papa! Two little baby goats!" cried Judy. "I must take them to school to show to our class. Charles brought his baby alligator and Rosa Maria brought her kitten and Ramon his pet rabbit . . ."

"You can take 'em to school in Florida, honey," said Papa, climbing into the front seat. "We're off just in time. Look!"

The air was suddenly filled with a flurry of white. Judy and Joe Bob danced about, their hands uplifted to the sky.

"*Snow!*" they cried happily. "*Snow!*"

CHAPTER XIV

Journey's End

O H PAPA, do we have to stand up to ride?" inquired Judy.
"No, sugarpie, no," said Papa. "You've done all the
truck-standin' and truck-fallin' you're goin' to do. The man's
giving us an old auto seat to put in the back for you young
uns to ride on. Lonnie and the baby will stay in front with
Mama and me."

They had started out in the old jalopy, but got only as far
as Stony Creek, Virginia, when the car broke down. Papa went
to a second-hand auto place, turned it in and bought a second-
hand truck. The two-wheeled trailer, now on its last legs, was
abandoned, and the goats were put into the truck. There wasn't
much furniture left. The bureau, table, bed and sewing-machine had gone long ago. Only the kerosene stove, the tent,

the mattress and quilts, and cartons of clothing and cooking utensils remained.

It was fun riding on the auto seat in the back of the truck. Joe Bob held Barney and the two girls played with the baby goats.

One night in South Carolina it was chilly and cold, so they stopped at a Tourist Camp instead of putting up the tent. They took two cabins and all slept in beds. The manager had a restaurant by the roadside and they ate breakfast there. While they ate, he stood by their table and told Papa how he planned to improve and expand his Tourist Camp.

"I'm junking all these cabins I got now," he said, "and rebuilding. The new cabins will be DeLuxe—the last word in roadside comfort—heat, light, Beauty-Sleep mattresses, hot and cold showers, everything."

"Junkin' all these cabins, eh?" asked Papa.

"We had a big wind last week," said the manager, "and one of 'em blew over. They're not made so good—they were just temporary, till I built up my trade."

Papa got up from the breakfast table and went outside with the man. Mama and the children waited a long time for him to come back. When he did, his face was beaming.

"We're goin' to stay here another night and sleep in beds again," he said, "free of charge. The young uns can play around and Calla, you and the baby can get a good rest."

"Why, Papa, why?" cried Judy and the children.

"I've got us a house," said Papa.

"A house? A house!" The children all shouted at once with the wonder of the news. Mama smiled quietly. Even the baby cooed.

"You're teasing, Papa," said Joe Bob.

"Has it got a floor and four walls and a roof to keep the rain off?" asked Judy.

"Has it got windows and a door and a chimney?" asked Joe Bob.

"All but the chimney," said Papa, chuckling.

"Where did you get it, Papa?" asked Joe Bob.

"Are we going to stay here and live in it?" asked Judy.

"No," said Papa. "It'll be a house-on-wheels, somethin' like

the Darnells' house-trailer. I've bought that cabin that blew over. The manager sold it to me for a song."

Papa worked all that day and part of the next. With the manager's help, the tourist cabin was mounted on the body of the truck and made secure. It had a window on one side and a window and door on the other. Papa built folding steps for the door and a porch in back for the goats. He built platforms inside the cabin for sleeping-bunks. Mama and Judy moved the stove and other things in. In front of the door they put the piece of Brussels carpet with roses on it.

"Still as good as new," said Mama happily. "It shows what good quality it was, a dollar sixty-nine a yard."

"It makes it feel like home," said Judy, "just to see that carpet on the floor."

"Now we can go anywhere," said Joe Bob, "and take our house with us."

"I'll make some curtains for the windows," said Judy.

They stopped at the next town and bought four yards of pretty red-checked gingham for curtains, and Mama bought a clothes basket for a bed for the baby.

It seemed good to get back into Florida again where the shiny-leaved citrus groves lined the roadsides. After cold nights on the way, it was good to be warm again. Like that first time when they came from Alabama, Florida seemed like Heaven, and Judy didn't bother about the names of the towns they passed through. So when Papa drove up in front of a two-story

[203]

farmhouse with a verandah on three sides and huge trees shading it, she was taken by surprise.

It was the Gibsons' place.

It looked just the same. The yard was full of blooming flowers and the verandah was full of blooming house-plants. Mrs. Gibson and Mary John were coming down the path with outstretched hands. Behind them came Mr. Gibson, on his feet again but limping a little. And after a while, Ollie Peters appeared, as jovial and good-natured as ever, and shook hands all round.

It was like coming home.

The Gibsons exclaimed over the house-on-wheels, and Papa

drove it under the same tree where the tent had been blown down. Then they all went into the big house and Mrs. Gibson cooked a delicious supper. Judy sat beside Mary John and they could hardly eat for the joy of being together again. The children were put to bed early, but Judy and Mary John stayed up and listened to the talk of the grown people.

"We're not crazy about goin' on to Lake Okeechobee again," said Papa. "Work in the bean house last winter was very uncertain, and we couldn't get into the government camp, it was so full."

"It's a wonder we didn't all git typhoid fever living on that drainage canal," said Mama.

"Why don't you stay in this section?" asked Mr. Gibson.

"What I want," said Papa, "is a little piece of land I can call my own. I've wanted that all my life."

"Shore," said Gibson. "Every man has a right to that."

"I want to make a crop o' my own, and keep my young uns in school," Papa went on. "This thing of gallivantin' all over the country and puttin' your young uns in the crops to support you—it goes agin my grain. I git plumb discouraged the way things are. I wisht I was man enough to make a livin' for my family. . . ."

"You are," said Mrs. Gibson. "You stay right here and . . ."

"I need help mighty bad all winter," said Mr. Gibson. He rubbed his chin thoughtfully. "Wife, how about that old Stansberry farm I was tellin' you about?"

"Hit's just the place," exclaimed Mrs. Gibson. "Why didn't

[205]

we think of it right off? That Yankee feller that inherited it won't never come down here to live on it. He'll let it go cheap."

Papa looked at Mama, and Judy looked at both and clapped her hands. Mary John squeezed Judy's arm.

"A family from Ohio bought it twenty years ago," explained Mr. Gibson, "and built the house. They came down here, winters, for a few years. Then the old man died and the wife went to live with the married son, and the place went to rack and ruin—the house fell over in a big blow we had. Lawyer Tibbals in Oleander told me that the old folks have died and the son wants to get rid of the property. He has orders to sell. Hit's a mess—been neglected for ten years, but if you want to tackle it . . ."

"How many acres?" asked Papa.

" 'Bout ten, I reckon," said Gibson. "There's a small grove of neglected orange trees that can be brought back. Five acres will be all you can work alone if you put it in tomatoes and cukes."

"An acre of beans too," said Papa. "I won't put all my eggs in one basket. I remember that hail storm."

"Joe Bob wants a cow and a mule and a cat," said Judy. "He's got a dog."

"You'll want a cow and a pig or two, and some chickens," said Mr. Gibson. "I can lend you my mules."

"And a vegetable garden and some flowers," added Mrs. Gibson, smiling at Judy.

"Oleanders," put in Mary John.

"Is the house worth fixin'?" asked Mama anxiously.

"Hit's a wreck, but you might could salvage some lumber out of it," said Gibson.

"We can live in our house-on-wheels," suggested Judy, her face beaming, "if Papa *can get the land and make a crop of his own.*"

"You're mighty right, gal," said Gibson. "You-all stay right where you are till we git things fixed up. We'll go see that lawyer tomorrow. You can work for me, Drummond, till you git the place."

"I ain't got much cash money left," said Papa in a low voice. "That truck cost me——"

"I'll lend you the money you need to get started," said Gibson. "When a man tries as hard as you do to git a little home for his family, I'll bet my last penny on him."

Papa couldn't find words to express his thanks. He got up and shook Mr. Gibson's hand.

"I thought we'd be on the go for the rest of our lives, like all those other migrants," said Mama. "Poor souls—the journey never ends for them."

Judy jumped to her feet. "We can stay, then? We can all go to school with Mary John in Oleander?"

"Shore can," said Mr. Gibson.

"Shore can," said Mrs. Gibson.

Mama said nothing. The tears rolled down her face.

The school bus went right by the Gibsons' house.

The very next morning the three Drummond children

[207]

climbed on with Mary John and rode to the big Oleander Consolidated School. It was a new school, filled with new faces, but never again would Judy feel the acute shyness she had felt when she first went with Bessie Harmon to the Bean Town school. She was used to strange faces, strange scenes and strange happenings now. Her vision had been greatly widened. Nothing that could happen would frighten or intimidate or discourage her any more.

I am a part of all that I have met. This thought surged through her heart and mind. As for the new friends she would make, *people are what you think they are,* Papa had told her. She remembered all the good friends she had made since she left Alabama. She remembered Bessie Harmon and Gloria Rathbone and Tessie Holloway and Mary John Gibson and Orrie Fletcher and Coreena May Dickson and Loretta and Jenny Darnell and Angelina Torresina and Barbara Delmar and Rosa Maria and Miiko and Ramon and Shirley . . . all the good friends who had loved her and taught her wisdom. Something of each of them was in her now, giving her strength and courage.

I am a part of all that I have met. Armed with her own goodness, she went out to face a world of people whom she believed to be fundamentally good. She entered the new school, determined to be kind to others *first.* This gave her the comforting assurance that the children she would meet would be kind to her in return, and become her friends.

She carried her beloved Geography under her arm. And

one of the first things she did, after Mary John told the teacher of her travels, was to point out on the map the places where she had been and tell what she knew about them.

"It's a good school, Papa," she reported at home, "and I'm in the Fifth Grade. I like my teacher and she says I'll be ready for Sixth soon."

"I'm in Third, going on Fourth," said Joe Bob, "and I'm learning my multiplication tables."

"I'm still in First," said Cora Jane.

"Pretty soon I go too," added Lonnie.

Papa was glad. "I want my young uns to know more than I do," he said.

And so the Drummonds got their home at last.

There was plenty of work to do to get it in shape. Papa worked on the Gibson farm until the deal went through, then they moved over at once. It was only a mile and a half from the Gibsons', and there was a short-cut through the woods, with a lively stream where Joe Bob could fish. While the men were clearing the yard of brush and vines and tearing down the old house to get good cypress boards, the Drummonds lived in the house-on-wheels. Papa put the tent up near by, for a second room. They bought a second-hand cooking range and set it up under a tree out-of-doors. Joe Bob trained Barney to help him haul in loads of fire wood.

Then for a few weeks they slept in the tent again. The men moved the tourist cabin down to the ground, so Papa could have the use of the truck, and the cabin became the first unit of the house-to-be. It was just the right size for a kitchen. Papa put a pipe down into the ground and brought it up inside with a tap on it, from the flowing well beneath, and Mama had running water in her kitchen.

Missy and the kids were installed in a shed of their own and staked out daily to eat off brush. Soon a calf and three pigs joined them, and a wire fence was put up for a flock of chickens. Judy cleared the front yard for flower beds and planted her first oleander grown in Pinky's blue bottle from Mary John's slip.

One evening, after the place showed a semblance of order, the Gibsons and Ollie Peters came over for supper. Mama and Mrs. Gibson cooked chicken pilau on the big stove, and they all ate at a table under the trees. They sat and talked until long after the moon came out and threw crisscross patterns over the white tablecloth and the white sand at their feet. The frogs began to peep in a lonely pond and a bob-white called in the distance.

Judy sat still, her heart and mind as peaceful as the scene. Then she moved over and tucked her hand under her father's elbow.

"Oh Papa! I keep thinkin' of Madame Rosie and the things she said . . ."

"Tell me, honey," said Papa.

"She said I would know hard work and grief and sorrow and dirt," said Judy, "but I'd have a book with pictures in it —that must have been my Geography—oh, Papa, the school's got a library just full of books and they all got pictures in 'em! And she said we'd have a little white house set in a garden with a picket fence around it. I never knew what a picket fence was until Barbara Delmar showed me."

"We'll paint the house white, honey," said Papa, "when we git it built. We'll make a fence too, to remember Madame Rosie by."

"How nice to have a fortune come true!" cried Mary John, clapping her hands.

"Madame Rosie called me a little scared rabbit," said Judy. "I'm not any more, am I, Papa?"

"I'll say you're not," laughed Papa, "the way you beat up them movie kids in Delaware! The cop told me it was the best fight he ever saw a girl mixed up in."

"Hush, Papa," said Judy. "Don't tell Mary John about that. I was so ashamed afterwards. I used to think strangers had to be fought. Now I know they want to be friends, just the same as I do."

"Remember Hiram Adler back in Alabama, Calla?" asked Papa. "First cash I can spare goes to him. He was a real friend —helped me get out of the cotton field by lettin' me have that jalopy and trailer. And now I got a piece of land to make a crop of my own."

"I made up a poem," said Judy. "Would you-all like to hear it?"

"Yes, yes," they cried.

In a low voice Judy recited:

> "No more will we roam,
> For we have come home.
> A garden and a cow,
> Two pigs and a sow,
> Twenty-five hens and a rooster—
> Now we'll live better than we used to!"

THE END

Wisconsin State College at Eau Claire
LIBRARY RULES

No book should be taken from the library until it has been properly charged by the librarian.

Books may be kept two weeks and may be renewed for a one week period.

A fine of ten cents a day will be charged for books kept over time.

In case of loss or injury the person borrowing this book will be held responsible for the value of a new book, plus processing.

Due	DUE	Due	DUE
JAN 8 '68	MAR 25 '70		
APR 12 '68			
APR 30 '68	JAN 13 '71		
	FEB 23 '71		
MAY 11 '68	MAR 9 '71		
MAY 21 '68	APR 16 '71		
MAY 22 '68	MAY 4 '71		
OCT 3 '68	MAY 17 '71		
NOV 2	JUL 6 '71		
NOV 21	SEP 25 '71		
DEC 2 '68	OCT 6 '71		
FEB 19 '68			
MAY 18 '69	FEB 16 '72		
	MAR 8 '72		
NOV 7	OCT 11 '72		
MAR 23 '70	MAR 21 '73		